Encounters In Igbo Language

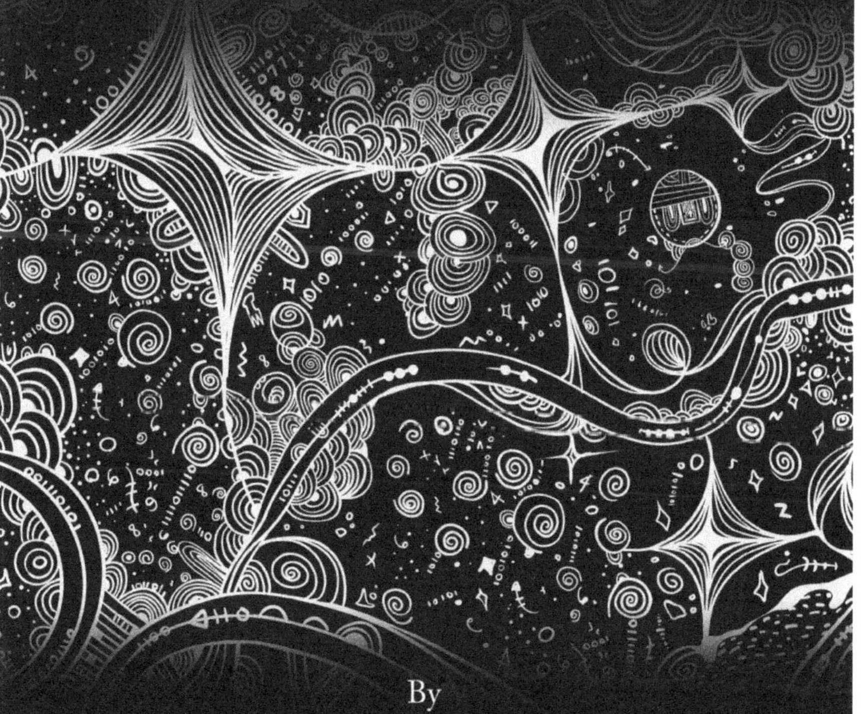

By

Alfie M. Nze

Introduction by Claudette A. Anderson, Ph.D.

Mmụọ Nkata

Encounters in Igbo Language

By

Alfie M. Nze

Introduction by

Claudette A. Anderson, PhD

Mmuo Nkata
by Alfie M. Nze

ISBN: 979-8-9935260-0-3 [Paperback]

First Edition, 2025

Published in the United States of America
by Unụchi Heritage Press
Tampa, Florida

Available from alfienze.com, unuchi.org, Amazon.com and other retail outlets

For information, contact:
Unụchi Foundation
unuchi.org

Alfie M. Nze
alfienze.com

More Praise for Mmụọ Nkata

The author presents us with an extraordinary vision: A dive, an immersion, an exploration of a infinite mental space that we enter through the spoken word.

Cinzia Vigna/ Anna Vox 109Z, Mayan Tzolkin Expert
Advance reader

An intense metaphysical journey into the heart of Igbo cosmology that opens a portal into the deeply encoded knowledge within African languages.

Abdulganiyu Rufai Maidumbayya, Hausa
Advance reader

An exceptional manuscript, it takes the readers to where the characters are physically and where they are in the divine. It makes me listen; and view the world from a supernatural perspective.

Lisa Clarke, PHD.
Advance Reader

Dedication

To my mother, Oyibo
Who taught me not to waste Words

"Ilu bu mmanụ ndi Igbo ji eri okwu"

Proverbs are the oil with which the
Igbos eat their words

Reader's Note

Mmụọ Nkata is not a textbook. It does not offer definitions, rules, or fixed interpretations. Instead, it unfolds like the language it honors—layered, circular, and alive.

Mmụọ Nkata is a book of linguistic metaphysics, woven into story and memory. It is a conversation between language and spirit, between self and ancestry. To read it is to allow meaning to emerge, not to be forced.

Here are some ways to approach it:

1. Read with your ears, not just your eyes. Igbo is a tonal language; its truths often lie in sound, rhythm, and breath. Speak the words aloud. Listen to how they feel. Meaning may reveal itself through vibration before intellect.

2. Let the stories carry the knowledge. This book speaks in parables, voice, and metaphor. Don't rush to extract answers. Linger in the spaces between explanation and intuition.

3. Trust the 'untranslated'. Some words are not meant to be fully decoded. When language resists translation, it invites contemplation. Read past the barrier. Return later. Let time do its work.

4. Accept contradiction as part of the path. Metaphysical truths often sit in paradox. This is not a flaw. It is a feature of the worldview this book invites you into.

5. Follow the signs. From the four market days to names, sounds, and numbers—symbols will appear. Pay attention. The book doesn't explain everything at once. Some meanings are cumulative.

6. Read slowly. Then read again. This is a text to revisit. To return to after dreams. To read aloud with others. To reflect on in silence.

7. Most of all—read with your spirit. This book was not written purely from the mind. Let it speak to your own spirit, however that manifests. You may find that something in you already understands.

Contents

Foreword XI

Preface XII

The Three Dots of Mmụọ XIV

Introduction XVI

CHINEKE 2

AGWO 8

NWAANYỊ 11

MMIRI 19

NWOKE 24

CHUKWUABỊAMA 29

JISHIE IKE 35

NKATA 42

ỌTỤ 46

ỊHỤNANYA 49

MMADỤ 53

OMENALA 57

ỊLỌỤWA 60

NCHETA 64

DIBỊA 67

AZỤ 70

EKWENSU 74

PostScript 78

Ọgụ Ọnụ Numbers Glossary 81

Foreword

In *Mmụọ Nkata,* Alfie Nze delivers a work of profound genius — a cosmological map rendered through language, number, and sound. This is not merely a book; it is a key to the ancient science embedded in one of the world's oldest and most complex languages: Igbo.

Through a layered and poetic dissection of words such as *Daa, Dibịa, Mmụọ*, and *Ekwensu,* Nze does more than translate — he reveals. He shows us that Igbo is not just spoken, it is lived mathematics, spiritual philosophy, and sonic geometry. Every word carries a numerical frequency; every sound is a spiritual vector. The Igbo alphabet becomes a codebook, language becomes divination, and the reader becomes a participant in an ancient ritual of remembering.

What Alfie Nze accomplishes in these pages is the restoration of Indigenous African metaphysics. His reframing of Ekwensu as a force of belief and transformation — not evil — is especially urgent. In doing so, he helps us dismantle colonial constructs that sought to vilify our deities and reaffirms the truth that our cosmologies were never built on the dichotomy of heaven and hell, but on balance, beauty (*mma*), and becoming.

This book reaffirms the foundational Igbo truth: *onye kwe, chi ya ekwe* — the moment one agrees, their personal god agrees. Here, *Mmụọ* is decoded as *M* + *mụọ* — "I birth/deliver" — a radical affirmation of self-agency and divine manifestation. Through language, Nze reveals that we are not passive observers of reality — we are its architects.

It is my hope that *Mmụọ Nkata* inspires a renaissance in the study and understanding of our languages. That it moves us to seek meaning not just in books written about us, but in the sacred codes our ancestors placed in the very tones we speak. May this book remind us that African languages are not relics — they are technologies of memory, tools of manifestation, and gateways to the divine.

Obi Asika

Director-General/CEO,

National Council for Arts and Culture, Nigeria

Preface

This book is best described as a "spiritually inspired" or "channeled" work. I never set out to explore Igbo cosmology or metaphysics. Despite undergoing two childhood initiations into masquerade societies, I saw them only as cultural rites of passage. I made no link between those early experiences and the intense intuitions I began receiving as an adult. At first, I resisted the insights. The messages were clear and deeply rooted in everyday Igbo speech—yet they revealed complex metaphysical ideas rarely explained in proper context. I even questioned my sanity. Why me?

To be clear, Mmụọ Nka+Ta(a) is not a conventional interpretation of Igbo language or thought. It is a personal, intuitive journey—not meant to dictate how Igbos view themselves, but to invite others into their own inner inquiry. In particular, to not be afraid to explore aspects of our ancestral heritage that may seem obscure and irrelevant. It took me some time and much encouragement to embrace the initially strange reality of Mmụọ. The method is simple: I make myself available, then write down what comes. It is possible to say that I am catapulted into the hidden world of the Igbo language, and when finally released I put down the information to the best of my ability. The messages don't arrive in meditation, but in everyday life—walking, bathing, even crossing the street.

Some of the earliest chapters of this book came as a thunderstorm out of a clear blue sky. I remember vividly the day the decode of "nwanyị/woman" came to me. I was on my way to an appointment one afternoon in Milan. While I was about to cross the road towards the subway, a voice came as clear as a person-to-person conversation, "Ghee aha nwa anyị ntị nke ọma, gịnị ka ọ n'agwa gị?...". The voice told me to listen carefully to the word "woman" in Igbo. "Nwa anyị" with such distinct clarity that I couldn't miss the fact that it meant, "Our Child". And, after stopping in the middle of the street to listen to it very well as suggested, the voice asked me "What is it telling you?" That moment began a flood of messages, disrupting my routines and causing much anxiety. Transcribing the voice/s have become my life's work.

This publication urges us as Africans to rediscover the depth of our ancestral languages. The intuitions come at any moment of the day or night, and I am guided by the new awareness that the Igbo language is informed by, indeed grounded in, the four visible market days and their invisible equal, numerals. Igbo philosophy, like technology, simplifies complexity for everyday use. Ancient truths were embedded in common speech.

After I eventually began transcribing the decodes and other information downloads, I shared some of my experiences with my late friend and researcher collaborator Moira Judith Mann. "Alfie, you are onto something very important here," she had said. But of course, I didn't make much of what she was saying. I was dismissive, not understanding the importance of what was being given to me. Then, Moira introduced me to the very patient Professor Claudette A. Anderson. Prof. Anderson came with the force of a hurricane, drenching me in her love of Igbo culture and insisting on the unparalleled value of the decodes. She became one of the major influences without which this book wouldn't have seen the light of day. I owe a lot to these two women, not only because of this book, but because I learned so much from both of them.

Here, I must also pay special homage to those without who I am not. I also honor my lineage—my parents, grandparents, and ancestors, whose presence continues to guide me. The first is my mother, Oyibo, my father, Agbarakwe, my father's father Nwokejiaso, Okoronze who was the father of Nwokejiaso, Diunamma who was the father of Okoronze, Diakubo that was the father of Diunamma, and last be not the end of the line was Diogbuji who was the father of Diunamma. Again, I Especially thank my mother, Oyibo, who often says, "Don't waste words as if you forgot how hard they were to learn."

This book aims to contribute to the current awakening among Africans, both in Africa and throughout the diaspora. It seeks to challenge fellow Africans and inspire them to examine more deeply the rich tapestry of philosophy, cosmology, and metaphysics embedded in their ancient legacies. Mmụọ Nka+Ta(a) wants the Individual reader to go into a conversation with the self, and for the self to explore and transform.

Alfie M. Nze

The Three Dots of Mmụọ

Mmụọ, commonly translated as "Spirit/Ghost", viewed deeper, represents the concept of self-birth or manifestation of the invisible "other" into tangible reality. The capital M=I. The capital letter M in "Mmụọ" stands as the noun or the letter/word, "I/Me" in the Latin alphabet. The small letter "m:+"ụọ"="mụọ" translates into "birth/deliver/manifest". *Mmụọ=Mmụọ*=I birth/deliver/manifest.

Mmụọ is the affirmation of an individual's capacity to manifest the third dimension/spirit into the two-dimensional world of physical reality. But there is more to it than meets the ordinary eye. As the letter "m" represents "i/me", adding m at the end of Mmụọ becomes *Mmụọ= Mmụọ m.* "Ihe di na Mmụọ m" is an everyday statement that simply translates to "The thing in my spirit/What I have in mind". But in the context of explaining the three dots, it becomes a revelatory statement. "Ihe" is "Light", therefore the statement says "the Light in my Spirit" and it cannot be disputed that "Creation" is conducted in the Light of God. Mmụọ= I birth/deliver, m= me/myself. Hence the individual is unequivocally making a divine statement of an inherent capacity to create-- I birth/deliver myself.

Mmụọ m says that we do not need a superhero deliverer because the individual is endowed with the capacity to create/birth or rebirth ourselves. *Mmụọ*/Spirit/Ghost is a constantly changing state and Mmụọ m truly represents the inherent divine presence of our ever-transforming self. To illustrate further, if a ghost/spirit manifests in a room/space full of people, it is seen individually. Even when more than one person sees the apparition, it will be seen differently, because each person manifests the other reality according to their Chi/Energy/Spirit at a given moment. If what we see is not particularly welcoming, the moment we realize it is only our projection, that it has no independent life from us, or that we are the ones projecting the vision, then can we change it to reflect the original state of the human being as "Mmadu/di/Beauty Is or inherent Beauty".

Mmụọ, Ghost/Spirit cannot exist without the individual that identifies or births it, this capacity of self-regeneration stands as a window to the three-dimensional reality of one person. Therefore, the three dots in *Mmụọ* represent the "three persons in one or the three stages of being" the individual M/Chi, the "Mmụọ/birthed/manifested spirit" and "the physical world" that holds both together.

Introduction

Mmụọ Nkata literally means "spirit of conversation." In this novella, these conversations are encounters—"encounters in Igbo language." The reader is taken inside asusu Igbo to experience its depth and mystery. The task of introducing this groundbreaking metaphysical realism is both daunting and inspiring, for in *Mmụọ Nkata*, we are treated to the very origins of human discourse. From *Chineke,* the Great God, to *Ekwensu*, the Chalk of Manifestation, seventeen decoded Igbo words illuminate our minds and refresh our spirits, challenging us to birth a new way of being from foundational concepts. The author, heralding from a long line of *Ndi Dibịa*, reclaims for himself and us the secrets of the Igbo language hiding in plain sight. The beauty and authenticity of the decodes shine through the prison of the English language, beckoning us to understand conversation not as mere discourse, but as Nkata—a basket, a daily woven work of art.

Nkata, this basket of decodes, masterfully presents to us diverse layers of Igbo culture. Each chapter is framed by Igbo Numerology (*Ọgụ Ọnụ*) and Igbo Market Days (*afia naano, ubosi naano*). As such, we are led to explore the relationship between numbers and letters and expand our concept of time as infinitely four-fold. The motif of a complete circle and the graphic of three dots representing the three-dimensional universe allows for a remembering of life as perfectly whole. The soundscape of *Mmụọ Nkata* is an affirmation of orality as primal; a privileging of listening as essential to wisdom. Original speakers of Igbo will, among other things, find great significance in the treatment of the letter M and the decoding of Ekwensu. Non-native speakers, on the other hand, may feel the book is missing a glossary. Orthography is part conventional and part received. Weighted by the light of Igbo metaphysics and cosmology, the book is open to all who will receive it.

Mmụọ Nkata is a story. It is the story of a young girl, Ada, and her initiation into her own Igbo culture. Ada begins with questions and, in the end, becomes a Dibịa—an expert in knowledge and wisdom. This ancient way of being, lost to her through colonization, is recovered and revered, with her now long locks an outward sign of her divinity. The interplay between questions and answers, the honest yearning among characters, and Dibịa Agbara's patient genius, complemented by the artful blurring of lines between day and night, physical and non-physical, past and present, takes us into a hidden multiverse, a forgotten reality. Yet more than a story, *Mmụọ Nkata* is a profound pedagogical tool.

It exemplifies how metaphysical realism can serve as a lens for cultural preservation, emphasizing language's role as a vessel of consciousness rather than simply a communication tool.

While *Mmụọ Nkata* stands in conversation with major Igbo-centered works, it occupies a unique intellectual and creative space. The novel inherits the cultural gravitas established by Things Fall Apart, which introduced global audiences to Igbo cosmology and social order. However, while Achebe's realism presents culture externally, *Mmụọ Nkata* turns inward, revealing the metaphysical and linguistic interiority of Igbo being, focusing on the Igbo language as a site of identity politics -- as metaphysics, philosophy, and ancestral code. By navigating this intimate, metaphysical terrain, readers are invited to reconsider the dynamics of language, memory, and identity, both within the Igbo cultural context and universally. It enriches readers by restoring ancient linguistic wisdom to the present and invites ongoing reflection on how language fundamentally shapes consciousness and cultural continuity.

The novel aligns with but exceeds the thematic ambitions of contemporary Nigerian and African diaspora works. None of these works address language as the primary philosophical and metaphysical force of the narrative. No current Nigerian or African novel positions language itself—as sound, essence, and cosmological being—at the center of its story. As such, *Mmụọ Nkata* creates a new literary category: "Decolonial Linguistic Metaphysical Fiction." The educational value of this rare blend of indigenous spirituality, linguistic exploration, philosophical narrative, and cultural reclamation is inestimable. *Mmụọ Nkata* is rich. *Mmụọ Nkata* is memory. *Mmụọ Nkata* is the recovery of a primordial language and the unveiling of a lost worldview. *Mmụọ Nkata* is Knowledge Reparation. If nothing else, may this basket of seventeen keys remind us that we are mmadu—beautiful beings on a wisdom journey.

Claudette A. Anderson, Ph.D.
Director, Unụchi Foundation

Mmuo Nkata, the Spirit of Conversation, extended themselves from the underground *Obi* to the *Ama Ocha*. They were waiting expectantly, excited that young Ada, about to be initiated *Dibịa,* would soon engage them. It had been many market days since *Ndi Ọbịa* had chosen this most sacred path – the path of *Okwu,* the Word. *Mmụọ Nkata* breathe the four sacred breaths and waited for the one who would come open the door to the world of words. *Mmụọ Nkata*, the Spirit of Conversation welcomed Ada and Agbara, the ones who had chosen, to have conversations with spirits--to have **ENCOUNTERS IN IGBO LANGUAGE.**

CHINEKE

CHI - N(A) - EKE

3+11+12 21+(1) 5+15+5

I

CHINEKE

Afọ Ukwu

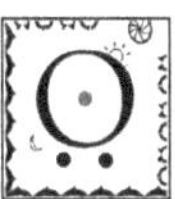

One evening, after Afọ Ukwu was traded and marketers from the East, South, West, and North—the visible and invisible worlds—had retired, dusk came at the door of night.

Agbara, the great Dibịa from whose mouth wisdom flowed like a graceful river, stood and stepped out of the underground Obi. He looked up and saw an image akin to a young palm tree dancing towards him. Agbara cleared his throat to inform the apparition that not a mere mortal stood in observation. The apparition advanced and Agbara witnessed the tree-head transform into serpents. Soon, the great Dibịa saw the serpents twist and turn into dreadlocks. He recognized Ada, one of his regular guests. A stool magically appeared in his left hand, and the great mystic sat, watching as dusk released its hold on the advancing guest.

Agbara stood up in respectful welcome as Ada entered the compound. Curtsying, Ada extended both hands and offered gifts from Afọ, the market belly that blends and swallows all.

"Nna anyị," Ada said softly, "Afọ said that Ọra, the Sun, is knocking at the door of abalị, the night. For even the undying eye deserves repose after a good day's toil."

"My daughter," Agbara said as he accepted her extended hands, taking the offer without unwrapping its contents, "Ọra's paths are familiar, yet our elders have an adage, *Ụzọ dị mma a gaa ya ugbere abụọ*. That is, a good path is trod more than once. Ọra knows no burden, yet repose in the mother's bosom is but a dance of joy. You are on a path known by many, yet trodden by the python, turtle, the sun, and a handful."

He carefully studied her demeanor. "What brings you today?"

Ada brows furrowed with thought. "Nna anyị, Eké, the wise python, crossed my path as I was about your home. I wondered then of Eké, Eke, and Chineke."

The great Dibịa stood and walked out of the compound, his back to the home. The mystic looked left, right, up and down and saw none on their stomach. He then examined the python's tracks and determined it was female. He returned and walked straight into the underground Obi. Soon, the Dibịa reappeared with sackcloth of Afa. From this sacred bag, Agbara brought out various objects: three medium-sized ọfọ. A fourth ọfọ with a huge base as if meant to carry the others and the entire universe. He brought nzu, kolanut, and various other beings that accompany divination.

With nzu, Agbara drew a perfect circle and assembled the beings—some human, others of other-worldly features—around the circle. After setting up the great assembly, he finally dipped his hand into the small spacious bag and brought out three more. The Mystic broke kola as communion between himself, Ada, the visible and invisible world. He offered one to Ada, threw four pieces into the circle and began reading messages as they appeared on the floor.

"Adam, Ala is never ignorant of fallen rain and the cock cries at night for naught. I will speak to your requests as the words appear —" Agbara paused, picking up a kolanut, he then looked intently towards the entrance of the compound, as if more visitors had come.

He moved each of the intently observing beings around the circle, broke more kola, threw eight pieces into the circle, and began speaking once more.

"Adam," He repeated, "Ala is never ignorant of fallen rain and the cock cries at night for naught. I will speak to your requests as the words appear. For letters have their own life, they disentangle according to the Chi that moves them. At school, you are taught different parts of speech. In these words, we have a verb, a doing word that they say, in Eke which means to create. It also symbolizes the creator and therefore doubles as a noun, that is, the word for a person, place or thing. But it is neither person nor place nor thing, yet it is All. So, this creative Force or Energy, called Chi, is equated with the Python who is also named Ekè. In this way, the first day of the week Ekhe, another noun, is the name of the day of Eke. Chineke is therefore commonly translated as Almighty God or Spirit. Eke means Create, Ekè means Python, Ekhe means Market Day. You will now see that the word Chineke is comprised of three words, Chi Na Eke. Na is translated as a conjunction and form that joins words together. Na is also a verb, in this sense signaling to be or to do. But these are lexical analyses."

He glanced toward Ada, who was listening attentively, eyes wide—not with fear, but with a hunger—her breath steady.

"Na is the invisible Unifier," he continued, "It is the reason we pronounce 'isee' as acceptance or affirmation of truth. 'Isee' is a vocal extension of 'ise', the number five. Five is an evolution of the four ways also known as market days or cardinal points. Ihe kwụrụ, ihe kwụrụ ya n'akụkụ, that another is Na, it is the invisible force that makes manifestation or disappearance possible. Because the cardinal points need a platform to stand on for their manifestation and that platform is the fifth consciousness. So then, Four is Ise, Five and Five is Four. This also applies to the three people of Eke. There are three but not three. It is four yet manifests as three."

The air thickened with awareness—as if even the breeze now listened. A single bird gave a slow, deliberate cry, then silence returned, heavier than before.

"Chi-na-Eke," Agbara spoke, his voice holding the weight of ancient knowledge, "therefore means the Energy, Force or Spirit that on Ekhe market day Creates, together with the Python; that is, the Creator, God or Spirit. Alternately, Chi-na-Eke is the force of the Creative Python. Na is the never changing Moment, the ISness of Creation. The ISness of Na is exemplified in statements like, Onye Na-eme mma, or in others like, Onye Na-enye Ife Ihe, Onye Na Chi ya and so forth. Chi is the Spirit, Energy, Vibration or Force inherent in all things, one with the Great Universal Vibration. This chalk and everything has a Chi. For instance, the Chi of the chalk calls forth the inherent Chi of Ala, the Earth on which I have drawn the Circle, and the Chi of the Circle calls forth divination and so on to the tiniest particle in the entire world system. My daughter, everything is preserved in words and some meanings are often hidden in pronunciation."

The Great Dibịa took a long pause. Behind him, a giant Nwọkwa—a masquerade entwined with pythons, bees, and various serpents, appeared. The apparition held mirrors of sun disks, moons, and a small basket of Chi, a huge Mother Python, Letters, Agwụ, Akara Aka Ikenga, and a nascent Eze Egbe-elu, the god of thunder. The Visitor walked from the mystic's left, stopped at his back and emanated a light so bright that Chi, the Day, was twice born. Ada blinked, and the vision, whose feet did not touch the ground, vanished into the underground Obi. Agbara looked at Ada.

Without moving, he nodded and resumed. "Be aware then, Adam, ah, these cleverly dancing letters, that Eke wụ, bụ Ekè, Ekè wụ, bụ Ubọchi Ekhe, the market day. Remember then that to Create is the Python, the Python is the Market Day, the place of conference, the place of confluence."

A light flickered from the underground Obi.

"It is Three that is Four," Agbara continued, his voice filling the atmosphere with a certainty that resonated like thunder. "The Four that is Five, the Five that is simultaneously Four and Eight. All is Egwu, an endless movement of the circle. So, then Nkata is yes, Art inherent in manifested Conversation, a constant conference of various Universal manifestations."

"So, in their eternal dance," he went on, "letters and words are woven round in the basket of Agwụ and move back and forth as their chi directs them. A letter could distance or join itself to another, according to the secrets it bears witness to at a specific moment, because naught is cast in stone, though even stones are empty."

He paused, the silence that followed thick. Ada held her breath, knowing that every word was important.

"What you just saw," Agbara stated, "was Ekè na Agwọ, The Python and The Serpent in the perfect, endless circle where the head is tail and the tail is head. Nothing is casual. Chi and Nne Agwụ were in the basket with Agwọ too. Nne Agwụ is Chi, Destiny."

Ada exhaled; the weight of his words settled deep within her. She felt her connection to something vast, something ancient. She could almost hear the hum of energy around them, as if the earth itself agreed.

"To some," Agbara continued, "she manifests as The Mother Holy Spirit, or The All-Mighty God or Spirit. But, look again into that Nkata, that Ekete, the Basket of Nwọkwa, Adam, my daughter, look then with your ears and you will see Ọgwụ, in Agwọ. This is part of the great mystery of the twin-serpent, the very riddle your questions attempt to solve."

His voice dropped. "As Agwọ-Ekè snakes her ways East, North, West, South, her movement is a universal law that affects all. Ekè births Agwọ, Creation begets Healing, so the Serpent swallows itself not... Yet, the secret knowledge of her workings, though preserved here at home, readily available to all who seek, is yet hidden in the plain sight of those whose eyes are widely shut."

Ada could feel her own understanding begin to expand, like the world was opening up to her in ways she had never expected.

"On this planet called Ala, where we have our life, she is Ọgwụ Ukwu, the Great Medicine, the Great Healer." Agbara turned to Ada, his gaze piercing through darkness as if he was trying to look into her very soul. "We say, Onye na Chi ya, each person according to the dictates of their Chi, their Spirit, their Energy, their Vibration. You have also heard me say, Onye nyoo Mmụọ, O hụ Chi ya. Ada, it is for all humans to find their respective

Chi, or God-self. Know that they are three people in one. The Light that their Chi carries, the thing that holds their Chi together, and in so knowing, they will live in light and may joyfully live the beauties provided by Ala, Earth."

Agbara stood up and peered into the distant horizon. Night had blanked all, and trees seemed to have put on walking shoes and danced happily to a newly risen breeze.

"Ngwa," Agbara said, his voice calm. "Ọra has gone into the bosom of Ọnwa, and though the Moon has blanketed it with Ọnwụ, confusing the uninitiated with Death, Ọra is only reposing in her belly. You can go home now, for Nkwọ beckons Afọ, eager to grind and consume Ekhe."

He paused, his gaze lingering on Ada, who was still absorbing his words. "The Circle is Always Complete."

Ada bowed her head in respect and turned to leave the compound. Agbara stood silently walking behind her.

His pace slowed as he watched her disappear into the horizon. He pronounced words of blessings and walked back into the compound. The mouth of the Obi opened and the Dibịa walked in. He glanced at the apparition and a forest. Both masquerade and forest disappeared as quickly as they appeared.

Soon after, Ada came running back, panting heavily.

As if already informed of her return, the great mystic appeared at the place where they had met earlier. Ada arrived, her speech and breathing difficult until Agbara calmed the young, troubled child.

"The earth does not run, no matter how frightful a sight may appear," Agbara said softly. "Calm down, Ada, for the eyes bleed at no vision."

"Nna anyị," Ada gasped, looking up at him with wide, desperate eyes. "They say an elder's wrapper blinds a child attempting to lift him."

"Yes," Agbara replied, his voice steady, "yet a child that washes their hands dines with the elders. Your hands are clean."

Ada, exhaled in relief. "I thank you, Nna anyị! Yet, it seems I am treading on paths too dense for my feet."

"The medicine forest holds no secrets to a staff properly wielded," Agbara said, his tone reassuring. "Your journey is well sanctioned."

Ada's voice quivered as she spoke again. "Nna anyị, Ekè greeted my journey earlier and Agwọ stood now on a branch, barring my way!"

AGWỌ
A - GWỌ
1
10+26

II

AGWỌ

Afọ Ukwu

O "You were sent on a double errand in a single day Ada," Agbara said. "Agwọ, the Serpent, did not bar your path. You were sent to complete the circle."

He looked past her, toward the horizon where she had last disappeared. "Listen well, then. For Agwọ cries out: I am the poison and the antidote. I am the Snake that heals my bite. For though I inject venom, yet in one tongue I carry Mmiri Ọgwụ — Healing Waters."

Ada listened, feeling the words not just through her ears, but with her whole body.

"Listen to her," Agbara continued, "for her poison is sweet medicine. It is the perfect circle. The branch she stood on is Mkpara. It showed you the healer's stick and you know he is called Onye Mgbọrọ Ọgwụ"

Ada nodded.

"Ada," Agbara said, his voice calm yet unwavering, "your mission is complex. Though young, you walk with ancient feet."

Then, as if summoned by the rhythm of his own speech, the great Mystic stood. A turtle emerged from beneath him. He walked once more out of his compound, however, instead of coming back in, Ada saw him resurface from the underground Obi. Speechless, Ada watched him silently sit, and then he opened his mouth.

"Mkpara: I gather, and I consume. I am the energy that gathers all. I consume the gathered and return it to the world as needed. I am the mkpara, staff that gathers all of me and for me to consume. And, that which I convene I administer as needs be. Sometimes I heal violently by mgbọrọ other times, with licking or caressing soft music I lead my healing dance."

He paused, letting the silence carry the weight of this truth.

"To the sick," he said, "Onye ga-agwọ ya ọrịa is sent for. The Dibịa incorporates the full nature of Ekè na Agwọ, the python and the snake, for he is ubiquitous. Dibịa is one who is here, Di or Is, yet simultaneously Bịa. A sage said, 'After God is Dibịa', because he saw the Dibịa's ịgba afa, the wrestle, the dance, the flight with the ever-changing name and divination: here yet there, living simultaneously in various realities."

Ada listened, eyes gleaming.

"The Dibịa ventures into Ime ọhịa Ọgwụ, accompanied by his third leg, mkpara, and branch of the elder root. And, once in the forest of medicine, the Dibịa communes with the inhabitants and kpaa or kpara, gathers as the Oshishi, directs him."

She inhaled, a slow trembling breath. "Yes, Nna anyị, but why stand in my way home?"

He looked at her, eyes still.

"It was a mandate to look deeper," he said. "It is said that Agwọ na Mkpara na-aga otu ije. And, it is rightfully so, for they are inseparable in the journey of healing. Was the stick on its own or standing on a tree?"

He peered at her, stepping closer, voice lowered.

"Was the stick you saw standing on its own?"

"No," she whispered. "It was on a tree, Nna anyị."

"Iseee!" he cried, smiling. "And is a stick not the handiest version of a tree?"

The realization rippled through her. "Nna anyị, I think I understand now. The story of the tree of knowledge!"

"Iseee! Ekele dịrị Chineke! Thanks be to the Almighty!" he beamed. "Now gather yourself, Ada. Let me lead the way and none shall stand on the path!"

Agbara led Ada out the gate. They walked side by side, their shadows but a dot on the road. The Great Mystic eventually stopped, allowing Ada to proceed. Trees danced and whispered, birds spoke, and the naught was alien to Ada's young ancient feet.

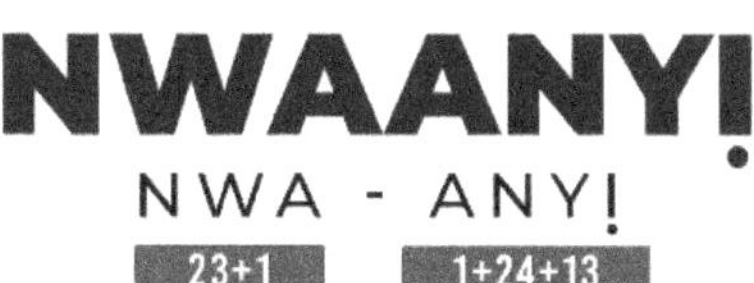
NWAANYỊ
NWA - ANYỊ
23+1
1+24+13

III

NWAANYỊ

Orie Ukwu

On a night and morning of Orie Ukwu, when all was awake and all yet slept, Ada rose from bed. She tied back the locks that overflowed her eyes, sharpening her vision. She tiptoed to Okechukwu — her elder by a year, popularly called Okechi — and gently touched his sleeping eyes.

Okechi stirred, cleared his eyes, and without much ado, followed her out the door and onto the road.

Their path led to the great Dibịa's abode. Ada marched tirelessly, her spirit high, as one leading a charge on a novel yet ancient mission. Okechi tagged behind, struggling to keep up.

"Nwanne m nta, jịrinu nwaayọ, why the haste little sister?" Okechi whispered.

"I have discovered a man," Ada replied softly, her eyes burning with purpose. "A Great Dibịa, in an underground Obi."

"A Dibịa? We are off to see a Dibịa in an underground Obi? There is no such thing in our land."

Ada slowed her pace, glancing over her shoulder, her gaze unsettling him.

"The compound is real. I have been going there," she murmured.

"Since when? This is not a journey for our years," Okechi protested, shaking his head. "Besides, our visit may disturb his sleep."

"Never mind since when," Ada answered calmly. "He sleeps not, and the hours are naught to him."

"But the night is meant for sleep," Okechi insisted, frowning. "There is hardly an urgency."

"For those that dwell in Anyanwụ, night has no darkness," she said.

"You have always been the strange one," he muttered. "I will not proceed!"

Okechi halted his steps. Ada turned and reached for him. She placed her small palm into his, and almost without realizing, he began walking again.

"The things you say are unheard of." Okechi whispered.

"Then prepare to hear words that shake the earth," Ada said with a faint smile. "You won't even believe that woman comes first before man!"

They continued in silence until they reached Agbara's compound. The mouth of the Obi was open, they stepped inside.

True to her words, the great Dibịa sat there, lost in meditation. Ada signaled Okechi to silence and bade him to sit beside her. They waited patiently for the Dibịa to acknowledge them.

Agbara rose slowly from meditation, showing no surprise at their presence. With a warm smile, he invited them to greet the morning with Nnu.

Okechi looked inquisitively at Ada as she took the offered salt, placed her tongue to it, and joined an ancient ritual by which every guest shares saliva through the salt. This way Nnu decreases and is consumed by the water that is human. Okechi followed Ada's example, handed the salt back to her, and she in turn gave it to the Mystic.

"I see she dragged you out of bed." Agbara said, smiling.

"Nna anyị," Okechi began, "I told her it is late — or too early — to be hosted."

"Nna anyị," Ada chimed in, "I told him the cock need not be reminded the day is at hand. I said you sleep not!"

"Yes, he is awake," Okechi said cautiously, "yet Father said not all that wake are to be spoken to. One may awake early, yet late in his calling."

"My son, you speak with wisdom," Agbara said gently.

"Yet not as wise as he should be," Ada teased. "I tried to explain Nwaanyị na Nwoke, but his eyes hear not as the ears see. So then, Okechi must drink from the original fountain."

"Nna anyị," Okechi said, his voice dropping, "Ada spoke, the words too heavy for her mouth and my ears. So, I begged for your meditation to not be disturbed, yet eager to pluck from your light."

"Ah, you speak from an ancient well of wisdom," Agbara nodded. "No disruption, my son, for meditation is for the living. Ada, what hides in your locks?"

"Nna anyị," Ada smiled faintly, "my locks are light, yet they dread my father's scissors, eager as a warrior's sword to cut short their lives."

"The wind defies even the sharpest of swords." Agbara chuckled. "Your locks need dread not, for they are roots of the Iroko. Tell me, which foot began the early morning's dance?"

"Nna anyị," Ada answered, "as Nwoke na Nwaanyị, the left stepped first off, the mat, and the right, as a good wife, touched the floor. The mystery of Nwaanyị na Nwoke made sleep and our feet lighter as sweet wind."

Ada handed Okechi a small bundle. He unwrapped it, revealing two little statues — one of a man, one of a woman — and placed them before him. She searched for something else, looking for a gift to accompany the request. Agbara, understanding, waved her still.

The Dibịa, still seated, rose and went into his inner chamber. He returned carrying a keg of wine, joined them once again. A deep circle appeared on the floor before him. The standing Mystic rejoined the seated self, as four became three and three swallowed four. Then one with himself and his guests, the Dibia poured a horn-full and offered to Okechi. Okechi touched it, then passed it to Ada. Ada rose, respectfully knelt before the Dibịa, and handed back the palm wine.

Agbara emptied the contents into a deep circle drawn on the floor.

"It is a lucky age for a land when children appear before elders with questions to clear all doubts," Agbara said softly. "Ụmụm, once upon an age, the Almighty Universe — the Eye that sees into all — became pregnant.

The entire systems of worlds, unknown even to their own existence, danced joyously to the momentous event. Eluigwe, Ime Ala na Elu Ala, and the limitless Universe rose and fell. Tumultuously, as every birth is an eruption of a volcano, the Universe delivered a child as bright as the Sun, Moon, Stars, and waters of known and unknown worlds. Limitless, a perfect copy of the birthing Ụwa, the Universe, was the new-born self. The Parent, proud of the extended self, like a tree her branches named the new-born Nwaanyị — Child, Full part of Us. The entire cosmos and constellations marvelled at Mma, the Beauty of the new-born; all paid homage and danced in supreme bliss for the landing of Ada. For, the Circle is Always Complete."

"Nna anyị," Okechi breathed, "it is a story of unsurpassed beauty."

"Do not interrupt him!" Ada scolded, elbowing him gently.

"It is well he exclaims," Agbara smiled. "For though Eziokwu, must stand in Ezi, examined and seen to be as clear as a pure stream, yet a palm cannot clap for itself.

Nwaanyị is the word that those to whom the mysteries of that original birth were revealed used to identify her. Woman, Ada. In Nwaanyị, therefore, Ụwa niile, Eluigwe na Ala, the Universe says: 'There is no division, for you are part exact of Us.'

So, you have Nwa, which is Child or Part, while Anyị is Us. This, then, was at the ancient base of Ndị Igbo identifying a woman as Ada, the First Seed, the Firstborn of the Universe. In other words, she is the primary manifestation of the Divine in this physical realm. Therefore, everyone, man or woman, is ỤmụAda, children of the First Seed Ada. For the Circle is Always Complete."

Okechi frowned, his brow knitting. "Ada, you said Nna anyị told it another way."

Ada smiled softly. "Yes, he did."

Agbara's voice interrupted gently, "It is so. I have told you several times, Okechi, that words have a life of their own."

"I don't remember." Okechi muttered, eyes cast down.

Ada nudged him lightly. "You are interrupting again!"

Agbara chuckled, the sound deep and knowing. "Yes, nwam, you will remember. Words manifest one way or the other, yet All Is as It Is. Oshishi nkwụ ndụ mụrụ ụmụ buru ibu. Nke onye ghọtara ka ọ ga aṅụ."

Okechi looked up, his eyes wide as Agbara's words thickened the air between them.

"It is also said," the mystic continued, "that in the Beginning, when Everything was Whole, at the Inception of no Beginning, when All slept widely awake, Chineke, ChukwuAbịama, God, The Great, Spirit, Creator, the Ọ Mụ, the Universal Egg, in one declaration, Ọ Mụ saw need to see itself in the physical Ụwa, the World, and thus manifested.

Yet, the Great Ọ Mụ, I Am the One, Me, though manifesting here, remained the One Whole Egg, both in the Physical and the Celestial World. The visible Self became known as Nwaanyị — Child, Us — the Indivisible part of Us.

Nwaanyị is the Sole, Undivided Universal Akwa, the cry, the roaring explosion of the Birthing Egg. She is Ada, the Venerated First Daughter.

So, you see, my children, the entire world left from here, and each tells the story as they remember. Yet all hail Ada, the Venerated. All are called in the dance of ỤmụAda, the children of Ada. The Circle is Always Complete."

A hush fell over the Obi.

Then, as if the air itself shifted, Anyanwụ, Ọnwa, KpukpaNdụ, Igwe na Eluigwe, Ime Ala na Elu Ala — the Sun, the Moon, the Stars, the Sky, the worlds beyond the Sky, the outer and inner surface of the Earth, the Universe — appeared shimmering on the ceiling.

Ada's breath caught in her throat as she watched Agbara rise, still seated, until his head touched the sky above. With graceful precision, the mystic fixed some errant budding branches of a risen palm tree, his fingers moving as if tuning the living world. Ada watched in rapture, while beside her, Okechi, to whom the vision was not granted, simply admired the beauty of the obi, unaware.

Agbara merged the standing with the seated, the one became two, and the two became three. The three persons in one: Onye na Chi ya na Ihe Chi ya — the Person, their Chi, and that which holds and precedes the Chi.

Ada, eyes though sharpened, widened in wonderment as the mystic went and came, while Okechi saw only the single Dibịa seated in quiet beauty.

Agbara's voice filled the space again, at once ordinary and extraordinary.

"Ụmụm, see now our mysteries made elementary. Once the letter M, mobile as the air, possessive as a jealous spouse, is united as in marriage, Ada then becomes Adam. Ada is then Adam for the father, mother, and all who identify her as their daughter. Proud then is Eluigwe na Ala, Ụwa Niile, the entire Universe, for it calls all of Ada's offspring, no matter their appearance, ỤmụAda, the children of Ada. Ụmụm, know you then this truth: The Circle is Always Complete."

Okechi's eyes heard, and his ears saw, so then it became clear even to him, child as he was. The great mystic smiled a wide, welcoming smile and continued.

"Some are allowed entrance into this mystery through the simplest of instruments. And then they marvel, seeing the indivisible Egg at work. So, then mysteries were naked, revealed even to the adamant sceptic and peering into the ancient mystery, they did marvel.

If a new Being in gestation is Ada, Female, it proceeds her journey in Wholeness, Undivided. Whole, as in the infinite moment, Chineke, curious and yet present in All directions, stroked and strolled Ala, the Earth. For an ocean is present even in a drop, just as the tree branch contains the entire stem.

So, Nwaanyị remains Whole till birth, an undivided part of the Universe — from the beginning without beginning, and the end without end. Because "The Circle is Always Complete."

Okechi shifted his weight uneasily, his face drawn in a frown. "Nna anyị, this load is too heavy. My head swirls!"

Agbara's voice came gently, with a firmness that wrapped around Okechi's worry. "You will be aided to manifest that which was buried, in you and others. For, the Circle is Always Complete."

Ada, glancing toward the doorway where dawn's pale light spilled in, spoke softly. "Nna anyị, school hours are at the door."

Agbara's smile was slow, timeless. "Yes, you must proceed to those walls. Keep your ears and eyes alert. Pay attention to the palms and their fronds."

Okechi's lips tugged into a small grin. "Nna anyị, the walls are made of cement now. Can I tarry for Nwoke?"

Agbara's eyes twinkled with the weight of old truths. "A path that leads to the new has its ropes in the old. Go now and let none lead you astray."

Okechi hesitated. "Can I come back, Nna anyị?"

Agbara reached out, resting a firm but gentle hand on the boy's shoulder. "Your feet will not lead you astray. Head you then to school and be patient, as the elder is patient with a parading child."

The children rose, brushing the dust from their clothes, and walked out of the dim Obi. The Dibịa, Agbara, settled deeper into his seat, eyes half-closed, sliding once more into the vast sea of meditation.

Time passed in the hush of the underground Obi.

Then, slowly, the great Dibịa stirred, rising from meditation like a tree waking under the sun. With deliberate care, he broke the kola nut, inviting the present and past to partake of the communion.

He stepped outside the underground Obi, his bare feet pressing into the soft earth, and there — as though called by invisible drums — came a procession. Men and women entered his compound. Some passed silently into the underground Obi behind him, disappearing like mist into the shadows, while others drifted by, walking past him and vanishing altogether.

Agbara cleared his throat, his voice low, the words of greeting and welcome slipping past his lips to those who had arrived scarcely a minute after his invitation for the living and the dead to share kola nut.

Then, without another word, the Dibịa turned, slipping quietly back into his Obi. Days passed. Eke Ukwu succeeded the days from Orie Ukwu to Eke Nta, until the Dibịa finally rose again.

MMIRI
MMI - IRI
20+12
12+28+12

IV

MMIRI

Eke Nta

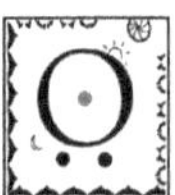

It was once Eke Nta, and everything had shifted into an immobile space. Ada had gone to school — and yet she hadn't. Morning seemed like night and night like noon. She had gone home, yet had not lifted a foot away from Nkata.

Agbara, the great mystic, sat floating and yet was rooted firmly before and behind the upper Obi. Ada found herself standing and sitting before him at once, her mind stretched between states of being. Then, the sage spoke — though his lips never parted. Eke became Afọ, Afọ was Nkwọ, and Nkwọ nestled perfectly inside Orie. All separated into Four, and yet all became One within the Eight.

The same circle Ada had seen on the road from Nkata now appeared again between the Dibịa and the student. The Obi transformed into the Amaọcha — the outside square. The outside square was the Obi itself. All space was but one, for all was round as Akwa, the egg of birth, yet the wailing in the funeral of death.

A child raised the head, peeped into the system and cried out for Akwa, for he was hungry for an Egg, being just landed. Akwa rose from one woman to all men, for the cries of funeral travels as far as the joy of birth.

Agbara's voice filled the space without sound. "Mmiri — water. Mmi — I, myself. Iri — one, zero, ten, infinity. Adam, look into the Nkata again. What do you see? Life after water; water after life. For life is constant movement, and the basket cannot hold water. Nothing can stand in the way of life's infinite possibilities because water is transformation. You affirmed I, Mmi Iri. You are the One, you are the Water Spirit."

Ada watched as his gaze soft, and yet sharp, as if piercing through the circle.

"Look into the circle, Ada, as in the eye of the serpent. Do you see the I circled by the O? That is the Universal O, merging into One, into All. That is the Universal Creative Energy, rising and calling itself Mmiri — Myself in Ten. Life is in water, and water is in life. Watch Her guide my hand, adding endless numbers before the 1 and the 0. I can go on forever, because this space is endless, yet it ends where we stand."

His smile curled knowingly. "So then, ten becomes the possibility of infinity — the Circle O. My daughter, may I ask you something?"

Ada bowed her head gently. "My neck can carry yet but a few loads on my head."

The old man chuckled softly. "An elder prepares a load for a child, yet must lift it first."

Ada smiled faintly. "I mena, nna anyị. May this ground produce infinite dust of yourself."

"If the Chi of the dust and mine meet, so it shall be. Ada, have you ever looked into a serpent's eye?"

She hesitated. "I am yet to gain such sight."

Agbara's eyes twinkled. "You dwell in the vision yet may not see it. Agwọ, the venerable serpent, holds the unsurpassed keys to vision. Look then into the serpent, visions are reality and in reality, dwells visions. Some are made blind to see, some are wide-eyed yet blind."

"Iseee, nna anyị!"

Agbara went on. "You will notice that when the serpent curls, it creates a circle — and from this, it raises its head, forming the number one and zero, or one plus zero, ten."

Ada's brow furrowed. "I don't understand the connection."

"The curled serpent and the raised head speak of the Creative Universe," Agbara said gently, "as a circular, singular entity that once raised its head to say Mmi-Iri — Myself in Tens. Mmiri invites us to look deeper. It tells us that we are singular, yes, but we are made mainly of the whole, the liquid, the One with the All. Do you see now why no one should reject the offering of water? Water is Ndụ/Ndu — life, worm, microorganism."

Ada's heart stirred. "Nna anyị, may I carry the water to your home?"

Agbara's face softened into a smile. "The jar is full and empty. Life after water is life before water. The circle is always complete."

Suddenly, the mystic paused. Without warning, rain began to fall on him — and only him — while Ada and the earth around remained dry. The mystic absorbed the falling rain, which then flowed from him to Ada and the fields nearby. Abruptly, the sun rose, blazing across his figure, blessing and drying the recently wet circle.

He laughed softly. "You shall be my water carrier. Pour some into the circle and let us wait awhile."

Ada obeyed, pouring water carefully into the circle. Moments later, a strange movement began — an inexplicable trembling, as though the earth itself was preparing to quake. Agbara and Ada watched as the dry sands seemed to acquire another dancing life. Calmly, the mystic raised his staff into the air, ready to intervene. Ada stared in amazement, while the Dibịa, unsurprised, struck his staff into the middle of the square and instantly quieted the trembling world.

The sands settled, once again dry and wet. Agbara continued his words as if the earth's shaking were no more unusual than a passing breeze. Ada looked on, dumbfounded.

"Once upon every time without beginning, the Great O — Eluigwe na Ala — in Ịhụnanya. It willed itself into many lands, and from that Will, the Great O donated a part of its endless Self. So then, every particle could be found in Mmi-Iri — Myself in Tenfold, Myself in Water.

The Great O became everything to every land. Here on this plane, we come to Ndụ as Aja, sacrifice, the sands of Ala. Aja, the sacrifice, the sand, is an instrument of divination, the process by which all is set straight. For sands are worms, and worms are sands. When an individual Chi — the part, the holder inseparable from the Great O — chooses to come into this plane, life appears first like Ndụ, like worm, at the early stage of whatever form of the chosen Womb.

So, shifting away from this plane of matter, the closest way to Ndụ is Mmiri, in all its forms — liquid, solid, flowing, or dormant. And so, the Great O sprinkled itself across n'Ụwa Niile as Mmiri."

Ada murmured softly, "Mmiri anaghị echefu ụzọ ọ gafere."

Agbara nodded. "O wụ eziokwu, Adam. Yes, it is true, my daughter — water never forgets its passage. Exactly because the Chi of the Great O is everywhere and never loses memory of its journey or presence. Hence it is said Mmiri bụ Ndụ. Mmiri Ndụ bụ Isi. Water Is the Head of Life, the first secret of Water as a symbol of existence was taken away from hidden circles and made manifest in that affirmation Mmiri Bụ. We must honor streams, lakes, rivers, and oceans, for we are water, and water is life. Water after life, life after water. Nkata, Ekete. The circle is always complete."

Ada bowed her head. "I mena nna anyị! I thank you."

The mystic smiled. "The mouth is not loud when there is no ear to speak to... so I thank you!"

Ada raised her gaze, hope flickering in her eyes. "Nna anyị, how many people can I bring to your Obi? Can I bring my mother, my father, my friends, my neighbors?"

"You shall move as you are directed, but yes, you can. I am called henceforth to reach an agreement with you. Are you ready?"

"Yes, Nna anyị, as long as it is not too heavy."

His voice was firm yet warm. "An elder must properly weigh a load. A child dines with elders when their hands are properly cleaned. But your hands need not be washed, for they come red, brown, and black as this Ala. Our pact is that you shall bring no gifts henceforth, for I repeat: The mouth is not loud when there is no ear to speak to. The circle is always complete."

Ada pressed her hands together. "I mena, Nna anyị, I thank you. Is there anything more to be said about Nkata, about Mmiri?"

Agbara's face glowed. "Oh, Adam, Nkata is also part of the endless circle. Nka can be seen as the resident force or spirit in the middle of this circle, like the various groups we just saw. Ta, on the other hand, is the constantly changing reality, the day, the moment, the flowing waters. Ta is the subject matter that dances from one to the other."

Suddenly, the scenery transmuted, shifting smoothly back to the place where the four roads met once again. The drawing slowly faded from view. Ada was no longer surprised at the transformation.

She turned her eyes toward the crossroads.

"The road ahead invites us," she murmured, "yet I will tarry still."

The great Dibịa raised his head. Without saying another word, Ada understood she was to proceed. She watched the mystic silently as she chose a path to lead her home. As she walked, the disappearing image of Agbara danced away softly into the distance — and as if he were no more than an apparition of the air, the great Agbara vanished.

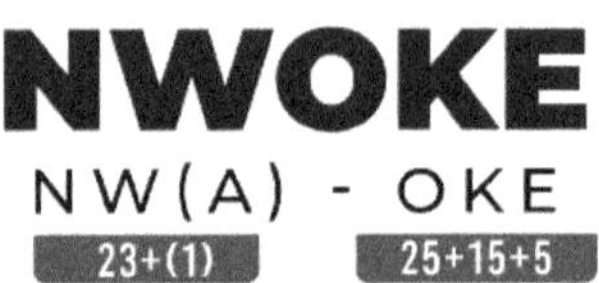
NWOKE
NW(A) - OKE
23+(1)
25+15+5

V

NWOKE

Afọ Ukwu

Days slipped past, silent as a shadow. Orie Ukwu became Nkwọ Ukwu; Nkwọ Nta danced its slow, patient dance around the infinite circle until it returned once more to Eke Ukwu. Major folded into minor, minor swelled, pregnant with possibility, until it birthed major again. The other, visible, lightly carried the heavy lamp of the immanent half.

A week was not merely seven; it was Four and Eight, for Four is Five and Eight is Nine. All that is inherent demands a body, a platform, a vessel through which to manifest. Some truths shared amongst sages and *ofeke* alike, other truths are hidden only from the *ofeke.*

Agbara sat at the mouth of the underground Obi. Beside him, Ada perched at his right, Okechi at his left — or perhaps it was left and right, for the center both held and released, grasped and let go, all at once.

Words appeared before the great Mystic and he spoke to his guests, without casting a cowrie, for idioms were pregnant and birth was painless.

"My son," Agbara murmured, "what is the Oke in your name?"

Okechi straightened, his voice small but sure. "It is Gift, nna anyị."

Agbara fell silent, his eyes distant, his presence heavy with thought. The air itself seemed to hush around them.

"To gift, to give, to donate," the Mystic finally said, his voice low, "you must first take from somewhere. So that which is given is a part — a fraction — of the giver, or of the whole from which it came.

Nwoke is Nwa-Oke, shortened. Nwa Oke — gift, portion, male. You are a child, a portion of the whole from which you sprang. So, though fractioned, yet by that token, you are fully Whole. It is the Divine Mystery. The Circle that is Always Complete."

Okechi's brow furrowed, his mind struggling to wrap around the vastness of the thought.

"To simplify," Agbara continued, "Oke is the divided part of the whole that is given or donated. In the beginning, when all was one, when everything was whole, yet All was also Nothing, because it was impalpable. Then, the Great Mother, Father, Eluigwe na Ala, Ụwa Niile, the Universe, caused itself to enter a stage of Ime, a stage of deepness, a stage of pregnancy...again."

Okechi shifted uneasily. "Nna anyị, I can't understand. Mother, Father, Universe... all in one?"

Ada shot him a stern look. "You are being impatient again."

Agbara smiled faintly. "Ọkparam, my son, you are separate, yet whole. Joined. When the Ime, the pregnancy, reached the stage of rupture, the Grand Ọ Mmi, Ọ Mu, the Universe birthed itself once more — Ọ Mụ, I birth, it is I, Me.

The Great Ọ Mu, it is I, caused a part of itself to detach, to separate, like the branch of a tree. The Universe seemed then like a grand catapult that protruded from underneath with open arms embracing the new world, Birth of Itself. So did OkeChiUkwu. To illustrate," Agbara's eyes twinkled, "look at your sex, turn it upside down — what do you see?"

Ada leapt up suddenly, her eyes shining. She spun in a wild dance of delight, her feet kicking up dust. Okechi stared, amazed — this was a side of his sister he had never seen.

"That's the Y chromosome!" Ada burst out. "I'm going to explain it to the teacher!"

Agbara chuckled, his smile deepening. "Be ready, then, to be suspended."

Ada blinked. "But nna anyị, why?"

"You can't teach what is yet to come from you."

Ada pouted, folding her arms. "But doesn't the child who cleans their hands well dine with the elders?"

"Yes, yes," Agbara agreed, laughter dancing in his eyes. "Yet remember — a child must prepare well before searching for the cause of the father's death... and a child must know when to approach the elder's table."

Okechi muttered softly, "Nna anyị, it may be my soup that dries my water."

Agbara leaned forward slightly. "Let me explain what has already been shown. At that primordial moment of Ime, Chineke, ChukwuAbịama, Universal Egg, identified one part of itself as Nwaanyị — the whole, indivisible part of Us, of Itself.

In the same light, the Universe called Man: Nwoke, Nwa, child, product, Oke, male, division, share, separation, donation of itself.

This would later be called, by some, by teachers, the 'Y' chromosome. But there is much more, and we may touch on it later. For now, I will tell you that it is the Y — Ji, I am, I yam — found in the phrase Ji shie ike — be in power, yam has become strong, powerful.

Man is the other side of the Whole Egg. He is a product of the primordial Egg, of the moment when the Whole divides, breaks, sprouts to become male."

Okechi frowned. "Man is the other side of the Whole Egg? I still can't understand."

Agbara's gaze softened. "You, like most men, will dedicate a good portion of your life, consciously or unconsciously, searching for that Whole from which you were separated. Some call it the search for the Super Female. But truly, it is the universal search for the First Daughter — Ada."

Okechi opened his mouth to protest, but Ada lifted her chin, her eyes meeting his, and his words faltered.

Agbara's voice dropped, drawing them in. "I repeat; follow letters; they have a life of their own. The letter M is the identifier, the possessive noun. It could be at the beginning or the end of identification. In Mmi-iri — water — iri, the number ten, explains infinity. And placing M at the other end of Ada, it becomes the universally known First Seed of Creation, the First Daughter: Adam. Every day, a mother or father here calls the first daughter Adam. Ada is the mark of beginning recognized all over the world."

Agbara's eyes gleamed with knowing. "Listen then, Nwam Nwoke. It is through Akwa — the egg, but properly the universal wail of emergence — that the old is allowed to become new and reborn.

Through Ibe Akwa, you are made to cut yourself loose from the Universal All-Knowingness, to emerge and create new experiences. For this, it is said old things become new. Yet the new is the old. For, the Circle is Always Complete.

Therefore, Nwoke wụ Nwaanyị, and Nwaanyị wụ Nwoke. Yet it is then proper that Man Bu, Wụ the female and the female carries the male.

There is no separation, yet there is division.

You are Oke — division, the manifest male aspect of Eluigwe na Ala. You are the fighting, warrior aspect of the peaceful Mmiri Ọma.

For this, Ala, Earth, is filled with more and more and more physical manifestations of the female aspect. This multiplication is to calm the other, the mirror, the male, the warrior, fighting the division of itself, the separation from the whole.

Once the male aspect comes to this consciousness, then will he lay his head in peace upon the bosom of the female self, and the entire cosmos will dance in blissfulness. Then once more, the Circle will be shown to be Always Complete."

CHUKWUABỊAMA

CHI - UKWU - ABỊA - AMA

3+11+12 | 32+17+32 | 1+2+13+1 | 1+19+1

VI

CHUKWUABỊAMA

Nkwọ Nta

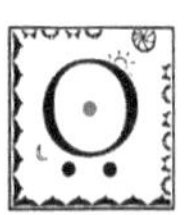

For Ada, it was a day marked by a long and purposeful walk. She had returned from faraway Nkwọ nta, on an uncommon errand for her father; that of purchasing the first feather shed by an adult cockerel. Sometime prior, Ugonwanyi -- another Ada (first daughter), only daughter for her parents and guardian to the family's wealth of birds had fetched the feather for her mother. She had fixed her eyes intently at an all-black, mysterious cockerel, and watched in total amazement as the cockerel crowed, more like a lion's roar than a winged creature's crow. The black cockerel opened its wings at the fourth crow, let go of a pure white feather, as if the weight was a heavy stone on its wings. Abandoning the single plume, the giant cock lifted itself in flight never ever to roost again. Ugonwanyi took the plume to her mother, who bore the sacred white plume to Nkwọ nta market.

Ada accomplished her task by buying the prized, virgin plume. She returned home in time and went to sleep at the hour of the hen. The dream of a four-year-old boy, haired in serpents, jolted her from her sleep. Ada recognized the boy as herself but could not understand the meaning. She had seen the python crawling up to a figure on whose laps the same reptile was resting. Ada woke, breathless, the air thick with the echoes of her vision.

Outside, the night wrapped the compound in velvet blackness. She stepped into the quiet, bare feet brushing the cool earth. Her father, Dikeakọ, the white plume of the black cockerel stuck in his red cap, was in the Obi carrying out duties of itu ogu. He was communing with his Chi, pronouncing words that made him stand, free of negative deeds. Ada walked out of the compound, without looking into the Obi, and headed to the Great Mystic. As night had deeply blanked the day, her father, protected by the aura of dark day, decided to guide her footsteps from afar.

Ada entered Agbara's compound and found him standing at the mouth of the Obi, as if informed of her journey. When he saw her, he turned silently and descended. Without hesitation, Ada followed.

Inside, the chamber flickered with low flames. The great Mystic drew circles of divination, brought out kola and broke them.

"You have come guarded," Agbara murmured, his voice rough with time.

"Yes, Nna anyị," Ada replied, her voice steady despite her years. "You said when something stands, another stands beside it."

Agbara tilted his head. "You have come guarded, Adam. Go outside and call in your guardian."

Ada hesitated, the weight of the words pressing into her small chest. "Nna anyị, is a child allowed such a task? Of holding the impalpable nyogo, the shadow that leaves out naught?"

The Mystic's gaze softened. "Those that send a child on an errand prepare the path for her. A load is never heavier than the carrier. Go. Call in your guardian."

Outside, Ada found her father standing, poised yet strangely halted at the Obi's entrance, as if he was being held from crossing into it. She looked behind him for others, but there was no one.

"Nna m, I have been here before, many times," she whispered.

Dikeakọ gave a small nod. "I know, Adam. This was the home of your reincarnation. Does he welcome me?"

"Yes, Nna m. He said I should come for you."

Ada led the way for her father. They both sat at the left and right, right and left of the Dibịa. The great Mystic offered kola to the new guest.

As the communion ended, Ada recounted her dream, her voice soft but clear. "I saw myself as a four-year old resting on the laps of a figure I couldn't see well."

Her father's eyes flickered, the fire of discovery dancing in his gaze — the understanding that his child, though young, bore the wisdom of an elder.

Agbara listened, nodding slowly. "Yes, there is a reason cockerels are heavily plumed, yet of short flights. Your locks were of serpents."

Ada leaned in. "Yes! So, you saw, Nna anyị?"

"Some shadows announce their owner hours, days, moons, or years before they appear. You remember that Eke once crossed your path here."

"Yes." Ada responded.

Agbara looked to Dikeakọ for his approval. At this, Dikeakọ bowed his head, signaling permission for the Mystic to continue. Agbara's eyes gleamed in the flickering light.

"Chukwuabịama beckons," Agbara pronounced solemnly.

"Adam, I shall not tarry," Dikeakọ rose, his presence suddenly heavy with finality, "two legs carry but one body, and everyone must walk their path. I will sit in my Obi now. Tarry then, be it four, eight, sixteen hours, or days, moons, years as is willed by your Chi. Nna anyị will provide a mat; you will not lack."

He turned, but Agbara raised his hand, halting him.

"Tonight," the Mystic intoned, "she will gain the two and four ways of movement. Of these times and not, of being here yet not here, of seven that is in three and eight."

Dikeakọ bowed low, his voice rich with reverence. "Nna anyị, the said and unsaid are understood. Adam, come home after the python's mating. The night will hold no shadows for you henceforth."

Ada's voice was a soft promise. "I will, Nna m, as you have spoken."

Her father departed, his figure swallowed by the night.

Agbara turned to Ada, his eyes as deep as ancestral wells. "Chiukwu Abịa Ama is the Great Universal Spirit. That Which Comes, Goes, Dwells in Light, in Wisdom. Chi is Mmụọ, the Spirit, the Energy. Ukwu is Great, the Base from which All springs forth. Abịa is that which is Coming, Moving, Going. Ama is the Perfect Wisdom with which the Universe shines light on all directions without distinction."

Ada's brow furrowed, the words heavy. "Nna anyị, this is too complex."

With a small smile, Agbara rose. "Adam, come."

They crossed the upper Obi, stepping into a road emptied of mortals but alive with unseen presences, those that appear only to the Ndi Mụ Anya, those that are awake to the Birth of the All-Seeing Eye. Agbara remained in silent meditation and Ada followed, missing none of the Mystic's steps. They arrive at the Ama Ọcha, the Square of Shining Light where the living and their shadows congregate.

"Listen," Agbara whispered, "with your eyes, ears, and nose. Your vision was of Creation. You were brought to Ihe, Ife, the perfect light, and shown ChiUkwuAbịama on Her throne."

"On Her throne?" Ada echoed, surprised. "It has to do with a She?"

"Pay little attention to words. Sometimes the tongue ties before some visions. Sometimes you are required to follow letters and hear what they conceal. Listen to the silent letter I of Chi-Ukwu. Vowels carry power; one is often too strong to let the other stand beside it. The ancients carried letters and flew to lands unknown to their contemporaries. Away from her, many know Chi to be Mmụọ Spirit or Energy, yet something is lurking. Chi is the Spirit that holds, possesses, binds all together. Gini ka ị Chị n'aka gị? Onye Chị ihe ahụ? These are common phrases."

"Nna anyị, the moon seems to be listening!"

"The moon has come to teach us. I will lead you till the four paths, then can you go home, for tomorrow is already today and today is in tomorrow."

"I mena Nna anyị! Thank you!"

"Chi permeates All. It is in the air we breathe, in the water, fire, stick, house, in a nutshell, Chi is in both the visible and invisible phenomena. Nothing can exist without its individual Chi, yet the individual Chi is an integral part of the Universal Chi. It is like a glass of ocean water that contains the all. Ukwu is Great and gives us a deeper meaning of Chi. Ukwu is the Base. It is like a pedestal that holds the top, bottom, front and back sides of a thing as it stands. Ukwu is the base on whom Chi operates and manifests Its Universal Permeation of the All. Therefore, the Base Is Equal to the Height, Width and Depth of All. Hence, it is Ukwu."

Ada watched the Mystic intently. "Nna anyị, I saw a yam stem bend as you approached."

"He was greeting the moon," Agbara smiled.

"He? Ah, yes! I am beginning to grasp."

Agbara's eyes glinted. "Again, Abịa is Coming, but it also speaks to the yet unknown. Na-Abịa means Going to a place where it is being Awaited, to a world where those to whom It has manifested are unaware. Therefore, Abịa is simultaneously Coming and Going, presence in different places simultaneously. "

"In the Abịa of ChukwuAbịAma ubiquity is made manifest. This is the light, the wisdom. Ama is the Light of Perfect Wisdom with which Chukwu operates All Phenomena. The Light of this Wisdom is limitless; it is as deep as the ocean. It is you, all humans and I. Mmadụ is the physical manifestation of the Universe as the mother of all, a full embodiment of Absolute Beauty. So, there is the personal Chi that is indivisible from ChukwuAbịAma. The only difference between the Universal Energy and the Individual Chi lies in the level of Awareness. Onye Kwe Chi ya Ekwe is one of such phrases that makes the complex appear simple. Yet there is another Chi in Chi itself. For even the Universe is held by the Universe."

Ada exhaled softly, her small heart thrumming with the weight of the words. "Nna anyị, I am not following well."

"You are, Adam. You are on the path. You usher in a happy age."

"Iseee!"

"Remember," Agbara said, his voice like the rustle of ancient leaves, " the nature of abịa-ma is She Is That who comes and Knows All. The AnyAnwụ, the undying eye that penetrates all, manifest and non-manifest Phenomena. The One that has the Power of simultaneously Coming, yet Going. But, my daughter, let us make no mistake, we are using the pronoun she as is known within these words. The ire—tongue, that could sell, could deceive or show Wisdom. So, the She in question is manifest in the physical realm in the Female body. Limitless and ubiquitous, Mma is the Universal Mother, the Perfection of all. She is the abịa, the creative force that simultaneously comes and goes from world to world, the infinite Union of All in Wisdom. She is the ama of chiukwuabịama, the creator, that which is expected to come in different worlds. Therefore, the word "abịa" can also reference "going"; as expressed in the statement, ọ ga-abịa. In this sense, "abia" travels / goes to deliver, to be higher consciousness and wisdom where She is needed. "Mma" then, defines both Mother and Wisdom. She is endowed with Wisdom of the Custodian, the One that bears Ukwu of Generated Life in this Realm. The Circle is Always Complete."

Under the light of the listening moon, Ada stood at the edge of her destiny, the child who was more than a child, the Adam who was more than the beginning.

JISHIE IKE

JI - SHIE - IKE

14+12 30+12+5 12+15+5

VII

JISHIE IKE

Afọ Nta

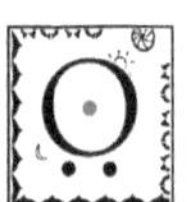

In the underground obi, dimly lit by a flickering flame, the great Mystic folded himself within a capacious garment and became Mmụọ, the spirit that births itself. He entered the state of Di-Bịa, a condition of Presence and Non-presence, where a spirit births itself to become visible.

From that place between worlds, he emerged at Ama Ọcha, dissolving into all: the square, the market, the traders of visible and invisible realms, the wakefulness and deepest slumber and was unattainable to common sight. He took his place in silent observation at a spot in Ama Ọcha — the square where many paths converge, where the physical and non-physical meet, where wisdom shines and truth sheds the skin of lies.

Eke, Orie, Afọ, Nkwọ, Ukwu, the Up and Below, Nta — the smaller, the minor bites of toil — where all traded, bought and sold.

Agbara watched Ama Ọcha and saw top becoming bottom, the invisible balancing with the visible. He observed the square and saw that chewed in Nta, small Portions became Nta, major Hunts of the falconer's laboured Game, where Ihe slipped gracefully into Itiri, its twin, the Darkness. Sweepers then came before deep night hid into nascent Ụtụtụ, Ututu, the penis erect that sends forth the dawn of light.

Abalị saa Chi, ọ tụọ ụbọchi ahịa — when the night washes off the garments of sleep, it sends forth day to the marketplace.

One became two, two became three, asaa seven turned to asaaatọ — the eight that is seven times three — a dance of perfect harmony.

A time at the back of time, then produced an erect yam that thrust upward from an airy underground. Shadows thickened; the shape of a figure emerged, borne forward with the yam. Slowly, the full frame of a man, Osuji, rose from the mist. The Mystic and the newcomer saw one another clearly. Osuji seemed mad by his dress — but what is a garment, if not a mask, worn for the self or others? For, isn't the riddle, does the cloth make a monarch or a monarch the cloth, but a quest for the blind? Osuji's robe was torn at every crease. With the erect tuber balanced on his head, he moved with the ease of one twinned to the wind. The great Mystic thought he knew him. And so did the newcomer. Yet none had stood before the other's shadow in their present form.

The Mystic rose, and the two men clasped hands in a backhand clap of three thunders, clenched by the grip of both palms. Agbara had never clasped another before, yet now, he did not release his hold.

"Osuji, Ji sie ike!" Agbara exclaimed.

Osuji grinned wide, teeth flashing in the half-light. "Ah, some greet me for I bear the yam seed, others for they see from sixth to ninth eye. Tell me, Sage, how does your front inform your rear eye?"

Agbara released the grip. "The yam directs the head that bears the feet. I see naught that your sixth, fifth, or ninth sense wishes not."

Osuji threw back his head and laughed, the sound tumbling through the square like bells. "Oh, wisdom! Ofeke chere na o wụ ụkwụ na-ebu isi! The uninitiated thinks the feet bear the head! Blessed is the sand beneath your crease."

Agbara's eyes twinkled. "The sand would be under a man's feet, or his face."

Osuji's voice lowered, mischievous and grave at once. "Do you not move at will from Eke into Orie, Afọ to Nkwọ, none holding you? Do you not fold yourself in the crease of your garment, birthed by the four ways like the mustard seed? So then does the sand reside in your garb."

"Anya gị dị imc, Ọ sụ Ji."

Osuji stepped back, voice softening. "They said I should come — that you shall be found when time inexistent makes love to time existent. And there you sat, Ikuku, nurse to the newborn, until fully nurtured, you make it the tangible sustainer of life here. Your children must know the codes you accord me in greeting."

"I bear no children of my own," Agbara stated.

"Yet you are father and mother to four, five, eight, and nine." replied Osuji. "You are that which was announced, and I shall speak, by the favor you grant me."

"Speak then" Agbara encouraged his guest, "for I am favored and care not for the glares of the square...though none but one can see me."

Osuji nodded. "None is alien that sees you, I shall speak by the favor you grant me. I have come as the voice listener, though I am Onye Ji, the Beholder, the giver of Yam."

Agbara: "Yes, and Ike is your Force, Power, Energy and Strength with which you Be and Hold your Ji, light as feather on your head, for to none is permitted unfaltering motion with yam erect on their head."

For a moment, silence stretched between them, thick as fog. Then Osuji moved. He leapt — light as the air itself, the yam upon his head unshaken — and danced, weaving around Agbara. Cleaners, unseeing of the two men, worked the square. Then, in a sudden burst of joy, Osuji planted the yam upright in the heart of Ama Ọcha.

"Anya m jiri hụ gị ekpukwele m ishi! May the eyes I set on you never blind me!" he cried.

Agbara smiled, lifting his hand. "Iseee."

"Speak," Osuji whispered, still trembling with the after-echo of his dance. "Deliver and let this square flow with pure fountain."

Agbara's voice deepened, as if it became the voice of earth and sky. "I shall speak, by the favor you grant me. You know nothing is virgin. All is known. Yet hidden are words and actions to those that speak and bear them. And so it must be for the joy of new discovery. Ji Shie Ike is at the center, as you have planted. It is the Mmụọ, the spirit of the seed that led your unusual sowing of yam at the heart of this square. Ji Shie Ike is the phallus BeHolden, Begotten by the Ọtụ. For does amụ, the penis, not deliver in the original intercourse? Mmụọ, the I that Delivers Itself or the Universe Birthing Itself."

Osuji, trembling with the urge to begin dancing, restrained himself. "Otu! I shall hold the dance, lest it drives my feet too wild and the world call me mad. MmỤỌ, I was well directed!"

"And so, we were both called, let us continue to circle the circle. The Ji you planted in the square represents Amụ, the erect phallus Nwaanyị na-amụ, nwa Amụta, Amụta ọkụ so it is a symbol of learning, of a new Light or consciousness, of birth or delivery into the world. Every representation of the meeting between the male egg and the female egg is shown in light. It is the Amụta ọkụ, the fetching of light. Surrounded in the thick darkness of the universe, the penis releases Universal Light to shine in darkness and pierces, penetrates the hidden realities, paves the way of a new Chi to take form and manifest in this reality."

I am permitted to repeat often and beg your eyes, ears and mouth pardon. These are evidenced in such phrases as, Nwaanyị ga-amụ nwa. Amụ is also a symbol of learning, as in such statement like, onye na-Amụ ọrụ. As a light bearer, Amụ is found in Onye gara Amụ ta ihe ọkụ.

The act of planting yam under the belly of Ala is reminiscent of the journey or the Light the sperm carries in the womb. The sperm goes through a channel of darkness before fertilizing the egg. And once the fertilized egg is ready, Nwaanyị amụọ nwa and the new-born sees the light. It is the same action of the planted Ji in Ala. You plant Ji in the belly of Ala. It goes through a period of gestation and once ready, the symbolically erect phallus penetrates Ala, the mother and searches for Sun. The light it finds above continues to nurture the darkness of the womb under and, once fully nurtured, the mother, announcing his readiness to enter the world exclaims in joyful labour Ji Shie Ike! At that, this square celebrates Iri Ji ọhụrụ."

Osụji remained silent for a moment, then he spoke, whispering, as if to unseen students. "So, Ji means to Hold, to Fill. A declaration of Being, a declaration of Essence."

"Iseee!" Agbara lifted his voice, a tremor of power in the sound. "Ji Shie Ike! Ji, the Yam. Sie or Shie, has become. Ike, strong. Ji Shie Ike is then an affirmation, an exclamation of strength, force, energy and the erecting power. Yam has become strong, it stands erect. And yet, it speaks of more — it declares that the yam has cooked strength within it, for you eat yam to gain a particular force."

Osuji's lips curved into a quiet knowing smile. "It is the mother beholding and recognizing what she has begotten, what she herself has become."

Agbara's eyes gleamed, a deep pulse rising in his chest. "Iseee! Again, it is also the amụ — the phallus birthing a child. It is the intercourse with the self, for male and female come from one single source: the Universe. Though you have wandered the globe, you remember Ama Ọcha, this sacred square where we now stand. The Gate of Light and its dwellers are known the world over as Yam Eaters. For that then, the most important celebration is the New Yam Festival. You were called here to plant the Ji at the center, because there is where it must hold! The center must hold! You have sown Ji ga-Amụ Nwa. This is no mere planting — it is a proclamation of divine truth: the phallus delivers as much as the vagina, for both are companions in the dance of birth."

His voice dropped to a hush. "Yet, the twin of the yam seed is not as strong or large as the other. One diminishes the other. One weakens the other. It is also one of the reasons this Ama Ọcha showed aversion towards twins. Because one took from the other what was meant for a whole yam, so none was considered full enough."

Osuji's breath shivered, a whisper of wonder. "Iseee. I hear it, I see it — Mmụọ, I birth myself once again. The sounds of intercourse."

Agbara inclined his head. "Yes. Your eyes hear well, and your ears, rooted deep in your sight. What you see and what you hear — Mm, Ụ, Ọ — the ancient dance, the mating you were called to accomplish. The planting, the intercourse between male and female self, the energies that begets Ji. You have placed yam into Ala, the Earth. In due time, the bud will penetrate Ala. By that penetration, the young and powerful bud will spring forth to embrace the Father, Anyanwụ, the undying eye, for all the world to behold the begotten son, the yam."

"Then every Osuji, the male physical equivalent, will tend and direct the erect bud, while the other essence is tended in the Vagina, bosom of Ala."

"And when Ji Sie, Shie Ike, when Ala's nurturing is complete, it becomes fully erect and Amụ, the phallus is birthed through the vagina of the Earth God. That wondrous event will be forever celebrated here in Ama Ọcha. So, in Ji Sie, Shie Ike, this square refers to the original copulation. That dance you were called to enact, that mating of the self, female yet male through which the physical world is birthed. Because both vagina and phallus are elements of delivery. Jishie Ike is a wish of Mma, Beauty of the created in the universe."

Osuji's gaze deepened, as if peering into a riddle. "A dance of the self: female yet male. It draws toward Ọtụ."

Agbara nodded, the slow, grave nod of a keeper of mysteries. "Yes — because the circle is always complete. You have cloaked your wisdom well, in a garb that confounds the uninitiated."

They sat in the fading hush, watching as Ishi Utụtụ — the early dawn — stretched its fingers across the square. And then, as if stirred by an unseen hand, Ada emerged — whether consciously or unconsciously — from the winds.

Osuji stirred, his voice a soft invocation. "Here comes the child, long crouched in the wind, birthed by dawn, yet mother to her own mother. She is among the handful who can see in this state."

Agbara raised his hand, a benediction carried on breath. "Ka egbè na ugo bere n'ihe — May the hawk and the eagle perch then, in light."

Slowly, both men left the secret space and were visible to all.

Ada walked up to them and greeted, "Nna anyị, ụnụ asana Chi?"

She placed her school bag beside Agbara, sitting beside him without paying any particular attention to Osuji's outfit.

"Father, have you washed the dawn from your eyes?" she repeated.

Agbara's smile deepened. "Ada, ọ bụ Chi kele Chi!"

Together, Ada and Osuji answered, "Iseee!"

Osuji watched her with wonder. "You should be on your way. The walls beckon."

"She can tarry still," Agbara said softly.

"Ah yes," Osuji chuckled, "so I was told — a child that properly washes their hands dines with elders. We were standing at Otu, the Centre, the vagina that births and holds All."

"Nna anyị, the drum was already beaten," Agbara murmured.

"And yet," Osuji grinned, "it must be beaten once more. For a good drummer tire not the ear."

NKATA

NKA - TA(A)

21+15+1 31+1+(1)

VIII

NKATA

Eke Nta

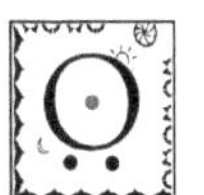

On a late afternoon of Eke Nta, when the few that traded at the less populous Eke Nta market were retiring and the Sun had shadows stretched thin like wandering spirits, the great Dibịa, Agbara, rose. He stepped out from the underground Obi, his sacred chamber, and crossed the compound, his feet stirring little dust. Reaching the red-painted fence that walled his home not only from the road but from the world, he paused. None entered here except Ada and a trusted few who bore special errands. To them alone it was a physical structure. To others, it was unseen.

Agbara turned left. He made but a few steps, yet had covered a thousand and one kilometres, arriving at a great square. There, men wearing crimson caps and red-and-white robes, and women in bright wrappers with high head-ties, sat in semicircles. Other groups gathered in rings, draped in every hue, the air buzzing with Nkata.

One circle passed ilu mouth to mouth, digging deep into the philosophies behind each proverb. The Mystic listened as a man threw out a saying; the others caught it, ruminate over it and passed it to an elder. Another recorded it on a wooden tablet, passed it to another, and so the proverb was chewed, its sweetness or bitterness tasted by eye, by ear, and by heart.

Agbara moved on. Another circle traded njakịrị, playful jibes that to the untrained ear sounded sharp, but to the knowing were exercises of wit and spirit.

Elsewhere, men debated the boundaries of farmland and the ownership of the plants therein. The contenders were called forward to expose their ezhiokwu, truth. Because only when each one's words are spread out, exposed and analysed in ezhi and, standing the test of examination, a word is then taken as truth.

Others were in heated Nkata, while others were as quiet as if in public meditation.

Quietly, Ada appeared, a schoolbag on her shoulder and a small jar that contained pure milk of the earth — stream water — in her hand. She approached Agbara.

"Nna anyị ndeewo ooo!" she greeted brightly. "Some sights, though rare, must not blind the seer!"

Agbara smiled, unsurprised. "Adam, some fruits, though young, come well prepared."

Ada's face lit up. "I often see these men here, sometimes under the rain, other times in the high sun."

"The spirit of Nkata moves and directs variously," Agbara said softly, "through letters, gestures, through baskets of hidden and plain idioms."

"Nkata is conversation, yet a basket?" Ada tilted her head.

He smiled again, approving. "Come, let us quietly approach the circles of Nkata."

They moved from group to group, almost unnoticed. One group of men throwing njakịrị at each other, friendly jabs meant to entertain, educate or pique the listening, all with the intent of exploring limits of the spoken word. Another circle of men and women were intent on dissecting roots of particular plants to determine their medicinal properties. A third debated the path of dreams, weighing whether a Dibịa should temper or unleash the truth. Some sat deep in debate, while others were quiet, as if meditating in the open square.

A set of eminent Ndị Dibịa, priests of undisputed moral quality, were debating dreams, divinations and visions, determining how a particular message should be relayed to the receiver. They argued whether a message should be interpreted as "good" or "bad" because of a receiver's immediate understanding. Others deliberated whether a Dibịa should exercise the same caution in delivering messages considered good as those considered bad. One group was of the opinion that a Dibịa must weigh the capacity of the receiver before delivering. Another circle was of the opinion that a third party must be sought as a middle ground between Dibịa and receiver.

Satisfied, Agbara led Ada away in silence. But before arriving where the roads show four directions for each to choose their path; the great Mystic broke the pregnant silence.

"Nkata is, yes, conversation, discussion, talk or basket as you wisely noted. But like the basket, it is a bottomless carrier of daily Beauty and the Art of spoken and the unspoken word. Like an endless recipient, Nkata contains Nka, Art and Ta, today. Therefore, whenever two, three or more are gathered, they do so in the name of that spirit by which what needs be said must be said and what needs be done must be done. Nkata is the spirit; humans are the medium. So Nkata constantly explores the artfulness employed by human, animal, plant and every living being on and beyond the earth."

Ada's eyes glowed. "I spoke to the teacher about our Nkata."

Agbara raised an eyebrow. "And what was the result?"

"He said he would speak to my father, that I shouldn't be speaking with a pagan."

The old Mystic smiled in quiet amusement. "Some have knowledge, others wisdom. Knowledge may come from books; wisdom may come from watching a bird change its flight. Wisdom must not be sought in four walls alone. It lives everywhere, in the market, under the trees, and yes — even within four and eight walls. It is found at the foot of a palm tree; it is present when a farmer, philosopher, medicine man and woman contemplate a snake; and when an ant snakes the earth and air."

He waved his staff gently, gesturing toward the circles they had visited. "The groups we saw are doing the work of Nkata, practices older than this land. In conversation, our people explore the ever-changing condition of the moment, the Taa-ta. Everything produced by man is art — from dawn to dusk. At dawn and dusk, we draw our circles, throw our kolanuts, and begin a personal Nkata with our Chi. In that Nkata, we mandate our Chi to act in all directions; from the one to the All. A task for my Chi to commune with the Chineke, the Universe. Whatever I encounter in the day is then the art of Nkata in action. That is the first conversation of the self with the All."

Ada's eyes shone wide. "Nna anyị, maybe you could visit our walls."

"I move as directed by the Mmụọ, the Chi of Nkata," Agbara replied. "When it wills me to commune with the spirit in the consciousness of Ta, then I will move as called. Nkata is the height of communion between man, his Chi, Ihe Chi ya, and the Universal Chi. It is the One that is Two, the Two that is Three and Four. That is the essence of the round basket — it holds no water, because mmiri, water, is always in movement."

Ada stood, speechless, wide-eyed. "Nna anyị, can I bring you this keg of water?"

"We are doomed without Mmiri," Agbara said softly. "Do you know why humans search for water as a sign of life?"

"No, Nna anyị," Ada whispered.

With his walking stick, Agbara bent and drew a circle in the dusty ground. Ada marveled at the perfect shape, the effortless stroke. They walked a few more paces, and then, as if they had never left, they stood again before the Mystic's compound. Ada poured the water into a small jar — a jar that somehow held more than it seemed — and then, they both disappeared.

ỌTỤ | **OTU** | OTÙ

OTU

25+31+32

IX

ỌTỤ

Afọ Nta

Agbara's voice rolled like thunder wrapped in silk. "Yes, Otu — the number one, the crowd, the group, the meeting — is also Ọtụ, the womb, the vagina. The Otu Ji, the single yam you planted, says one is equal to zero when stranded in a desert of nothingness. Therefore, Ji needs Ala, one needs place, needs others, for its existence. Even the one who claims the title of number one in any endeavor relies on the crowd, the competitors, to affirm their position."

Ada, wide-eyed, bent over, taking her schoolbook out of her bag. She opened the book and started to make notes, her pencil scratching with urgency. "One plus zero equals zero, but one and zero together, that's ten, instead of just one."

Her brow furrowed in thought, a spark of wonder lighting her face.

Agbara smiled, eyes crinkling. "Imagine, Ada, you arrive at school on the day they give the prize for being number one. You stand there, waiting for the announcement, but there is no one else. No number two, no three, no four. No crowd behind you to witness, to recognize you as first. And as you wait, nature calls, but the place of release is away from the line."

Osuji's grin stretched broad and mischievous. "And here, Ada, is born a dilemma: do you leave and lose your position, or stay and lose your dignity?"

Agbara's laugh rumbled from deep in his chest. "Iseee! If there is no one behind, no one besides, you cannot leave — or you lose Otu, your number one position! One need others to affirm its presence. One, I, O, M is nothing without others. So, Otu teaches that if a group is tightly bound, if a crowd, let's say even a small army, moves with a united spirit, becoming Otu, they can bring down a disunited opponent a million-fold larger.

Finally, for a decision arrived at in this Ama Ọcha to be truly accepted, everyone is called to rectification by a shout of Igbo Kwenu, Igbo Kwezuonu! It is the affirmation that the entire gathering has become Otu. And then, Otu stands equal to the multitude, for all pass-through Otu. The circle is always complete."

Osuji's voice came like a breath of light, his eyes shimmering. "Iseee! Ihe a wụ ihe a na-akpọ Ịhụnanya, this is the light we call love."

Ada's pencil paused. She looked up, her voice as soft as a sunrise. "What your eyes see in the other. Nna anyị... can you speak of Ịhụnanya?"

As dawn spilled its gold across the square, the yam stood upright at the heart of Ama Ọcha — a promise of light, a whisper of birth, a song that the world had not yet finished singing.

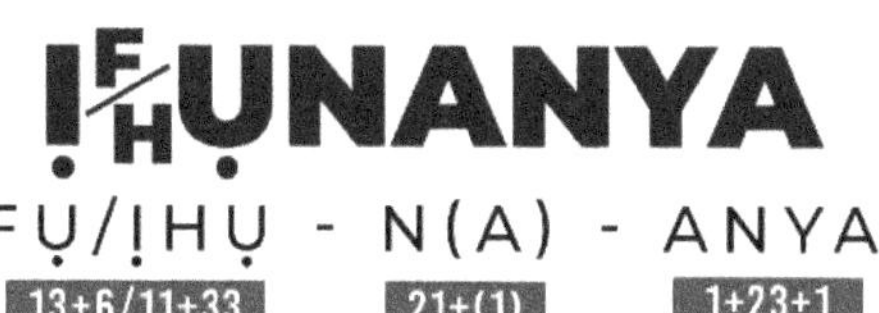

ỊF/HỤNANYA
ỊFỤ/ỊHỤ - N(A) - ANYA
13+6/11+33
21+(1)
1+23+1

X

ỊHỤNANYA

Nkwọ Ukwu

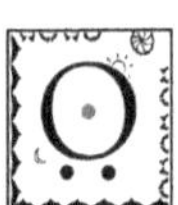

Afọ Nta became Nkwọ Ukwu and found a crowd of school age children; adolescents and elders formed a semicircle in the Ama Ọcha. Ada sat to the right of Agbara, Osuji to his left and the Mystic sat in the midst of all.

When Agbara spoke, his words rippled through the air, reaching each ear, each heart, each person understanding according to their place in the circle.

"Ịfụ, Ịhụ — as we see one another here, now." Agbara's hands swept gently before him. "Ịhụ, Ịfụ, are our faces turned as they stand before the moon and the sun. Na unites Ihu na Anya, the face and the eye, for the eye, sits deep within the face, permits the face to see. I see you with my own eyes. So, each of us sees the other according to their own sight."

"It's what the eye sees that the Obi, the heart, loves." Osuji interjected.

"Iseee!" Agbara's voice rolled. "Ịhụnanya it is what we see in the other, the MmaDụ, the person. MmaDụ affirms the entire essence of the human being. Mma is beauty. Dụ is. Together. MmaDụ means beauty is. This beauty is the essence, the perfect state of being, the Ọma of the Human Being. So, the human being becomes an expression of the universal I and Wụ — Iwu, or law. You are law."

From the crowd, Okechi's voice rang out again, eager and bright. "Ịfụnanya is therefore Compassion too. Ị wụ Iwu, you are, you are law!"

Agbara turned to him, his eyes filled with warmth. "Not only that, my son. In Ịhụnanya, there is compassion. There is philanthropy, donating selflessly knowing that doing to the other means doing to the self. Onye na-arụ Mmadụ aka, na-arụ onwe ya. Ịhụnanya is to see the other, the beloved, with the internal eye of Mma. Therefore, love."

Ada's pencil paused, her lips forming the question before it crossed her tongue. "If Ịhụnanya is beauty, then... that's why they say it's in the eye of the beholder?"

"You look into the other!" Agbara stated. "The eye is the window to the Mmụọ of Mmadụ. When you look deeply, into the other you see Mmadụ, the dwelling place of Beauty, yourself."

Osuji's voice spoke again. "The temple of the moon and sun."

"Yes," Agbara continued, "for the eyes reflect the first rays. They are among the first things we see in each other's face."

"Love at first sight!" Ada burst, her face glowing.

Agbara laughed gently. "We are drawn into Ịhụnanya by the face, the surface. Then the observer looks deeper into the other's Anya — like a space-probing instrument — to see what lay beneath the Surface. If what they find has substance, and, though some are hidden in hubris, everyone has substance. If the observed draw their life's stream from that deeper fount, harmony then reigns. And, since the lover focus is on reaching the chi of the MmaDụ in question, the lover expects nothing in return, because while honouring the other, the lover is recognizing theirs."

Osuji leaned forward. "What if the beloved gravitates on ego's surface and hubris reigns? What if the beloved thinks it's all about them? What if the loved thinks the lover's life or happiness depends on them?"

Agbara's eyes grew still. "Then the lover withdraws the power they once gave. The beloved becomes then like an object of adoration that has lost its power on the adept. Arụshi kpaa nganga, e goshi ya oshishi e jiri kpụọ ya reinforces Ịhụnanya. It is the observer who grants power to the observed."

"So, it's how the lover sees the other — daughter, son, mother, father, sister, brother, woman, man, child or whatever sphere of relations, all from the singular eye of beauty, therefore love."

"Yes," Agbara said, his voice a soft drumbeat, "because love is pure. Ịhụnanya is unjudging. It expects nothing in return. The beholder sees that which appeals to them from the inner eye. It sees the real state of being, the resident Chi that which holds the Mma is the transforms into pure Love. To illustrate further: I exalt the Beloved and I do not see, or do not take into consideration their weaknesses and even the requital of that Ịhụnanya. For, I am the Seer, the Generator that empowers the beloved. I see Pure Beauty for which I express Love. I bestow on the other this sentiment of mine, this Love for spiritual, yet physical Beauty."

"Ịfụnanya is Love for and a recognition of Beauty, which as Ada said, is generally said to be in the eyes of the beholder. It is a call to see the other from and in your own Eyes, to view them as yourself. Ịhụnanya is the deeper meaning of Compassion. You are doing to Yourself while doing to the Other. Because the other is a mirror that reflects you."

Ada, wide-eyed, breathed, "And so, love... is a mirror."

Osuji eyes met hers. "For, love needs a pedestal, a place to be placed on. What am I without the Otu? This is how one plus zero equals one?"

Agbara's gaze swept over the gathering. "Yes... Ịhụnanya is a circle. It is that which You see in the Other, therefore the Beloved is the lover, and the lover is the Beloved. It is two yet one. If the beloved drinks from the fountain of inner being, no reciprocity is needed, for their presence is enough. Because of the simple presence of the other, residing in full essence is enough requital. But, if the Beloved goes off rail and navigates a narcissistic exaltation of the ego, the lover will pull off the platform on which the ego stands. When that happens, what takes place is, Chi o Jiji. A fitting darkening of the energy or what was once aptly entitled as a Nightfall of the Gods."

His voice softened to a whisper that still carried to the edges of the Ama Ọcha. "Because the circle is always complete."

MMADỤ/Ị
MMA - DỤ/DỊ
20+1
4+33/13

XI

MMADỤ

Orie Ukwu

O A woman, Chidimma, mother to Ada and Okechi, wife to Dikeakọ, rose from the Otu and addressed the great Dibịa. Chidimma, like her husband, had long been an avid drinker of the wise waters Ada often brought home from the underground Obi. Word traveled like smoke on a dry wind that the Mystic and an unknown mad-looking man sat at Ama Ọcha in revelation. Chidimma, Dikeakọ, and every head brought its foot to the square. It was an Otu of unprecedented greatness, a gathering where all were kin—except Osuji, whose presence there was mystery to all.

Ama Ọcha pulsed with life in countless spheres. A towering palm and an equally massive kolanut tree surrounded a giant Iroko. Clinging unto each other, the trio's hands seemed to extend into every household. At the belly of the Iroko sat Agbara, mouth to a wondrous underground. The great Mystic was flanked by Ada to the right, Osuji to the left, yet both seemed to shift continuously, seated right and left at once, drawn into the shifting center that held all. The Dibịa was the Center, and the Center itself was the mouth of the eternally open semicircle, each dancing in pure harmony.

Chidimma stepped forward, up to the three-trunked tree of Otu, and deposited a tuber of Ji at its foot. Agbara looked to Osuji, and the latter stretched forth a hand, long as a tree, to take the tuber of gratitude.

Chidimma's voice lifted, strong and sure. "Nna anyị, it is said that at the teaching of the fool, the wise learn."

A soft smile, as ageless as the sky, touched Agbara's lips. "Nne ọma, your fountain shall never dry."

"Nna anyị, your loins will forever breed wisdom! My ears heard and my mouth thirst, my feet set on a dance and Mmadụ was the drummer."

Agbara's laughter was low, like water running over stones. "A child's extended hand is never left with nothing, and a thirsty mouth always finds Iyi Ọma. Though some feet dance not yet the drummer kills not Ikuku — blood vessel of sound. For, the rains fail not to inform Ala of their visit!"

Osuji's voice came sudden and sharp, a chord struck on the air. "Oh, lyric, oh music that the lame swears at his immobile limbs!"

The wind rose. The three trees in one rose in dance. Agbara rose, as did Ada and Osuji, and they moved — they danced — with the elements, their bodies weaving a tapestry of earth and sky. Sweetly, like the hush after a storm, they settled again, and the Otu, the gathered assembly, rose and sat as one, in harmony that wrapped around the three like a woven cloth.

Agbara's voice, when it came again, was like the pulse of the land itself. "Once, when the Great One birthed Itself and declared Nwaanyị an undivided part of the Whole, the Great Chi, the infinite Universal Energy, saw that the extended part is of an unimaginable Mma. Overwhelmed with bliss, the Great Ama, the Wisdom, cried out: MmaDụ! And as it sang, the entire universe, Ụwa Niile, rose Egbe Elu, thunderstorms, Earth and Heaven-quakes, in Egwu, A Dance of pure Bliss."

From the crowd, another figure emerged — Mmadụawụchi, second wife to Dikeakọ, third sister to Chidimma. She danced forward in circles and flew like a thousand butterflies and deposited offerings before the great Tree.

Her voice rang out, bright with passion. "Heaven quakes! Hold still my feet, that I may not sprout wings and fly farther than my body can land!"

Agbara's eyes glimmered. "Nothing is given to a receiver unprepared."

Mmadụawụchi lifted her chin, a satisfied smile tugging corners of her mouth. "I am ready; we are ready! Kọọrọ anyị egwu Mmụọ! Play for us then the tunes of the Spirit, hidden for ages — for the age is here!"

A deep chuckle rolled from Agbara's chest. "Ah, but a drum already beats."

Osuji's voice slipped in, smooth and sly. "And yet it must beat again, for a good drummer never tires the ear."

Agbara turned, his gaze resting upon Mmadụawụchi as though seeing through her skin into the trembling core beneath.

"Isee," he murmured, his voice a benediction. "I mena Nne anyị, I shall speak as directed!"

He rose, arms spread, voice rising with the wind. "At that moment of new births, the Great Chi, overcome with bliss, proclaimed the presence of pure beauty: MmaDụ! Mma — Mother, Beauty; Dụ means Is, is means Human Being. So, the Great One mirrored

Itself and proclaimed the Self MmaDụ. The Human Being is Mother, is Beauty — full embodiment of the infinite of the universe. In MmaDụ, the Great One planted on this plane, on Ala, Being that expresses the full potential of Universal Mma, the capacity to birth Beauty by Isness of actions. This capacity can only be viewed through the actions of MmaDụ on Ala. Your feet move to Egwu, powerful emanation of Mmadụ, full Beingness of the Universal Beauty."

His voice deepened, echoing like a drum beneath the earth. "Everything on Ala manifests as Ome n'Ala — the doer and their deeds on earth, pure bliss. Therefore, when Mmadụ's actions correspond to this calling, harmony is celebrated. But when Mmadụ goes off rail and their Ome go contrary to Ala, the supreme mission of blissful existence is violated, and shadows are cast on earth. Oceans, rivers and forests will run dry as of old, and sages will withdraw underground."

Ada's voice was soft, yet it carried across the square. "Our actions, then, are the only thing that counts."

Agbara turned to her. "Isee, Adam. It is Ome n'Ala: the doer and their deeds on earth. Mmadụ's actions move streams, lakes, rivers, oceans, forests, anthills, and mountains. Deeds are the heart that drives the mobile earth in one or another direction. MmaDụ is the mother, begetter of beauty that is. The true nature of the universe. Because the circle is always complete."

OMENALA

OME - N(A) - ALA

25+19+5 21+(1) 1+18+1

XII

OMENALA

Eke Ukwu

Thunderstorms raged across the land. Thunder flashed, gales tore through the forests, and the days danced by in a whirl of transformations — Eke Ukwu became endlessly Nkwọ Nta; Nkwọ Ukwu became Afọ Nta and Orie Ukwu. None of the days were alike, and yet each mirrored the other.

And still, at the heart of it all, the great Mystic sat unmoving in the square, at Otu in Nkata. Agbara was still and yet everywhere — from the underground Obi to the wild forests, from the bustling markets to family reunions.

It was then that Okeorie rose from the Otu. The great-great-great-great grandfather, the grand uncle of Ada, leaned on his third and fourth legs and walked across the gathered congregation. He bowed before the mighty Tree, extending his arms, offering a kolanut.

"Oke Nwoke," Okeorie intoned, his voice rasping like the wind through old leaves, "a sị ihe onye metara dịrị ya. To each the consequences of their actions!"

"Iseee!" Agbara's voice rolled forth, a low thunder in the bones of the earth.

Okeorie's gaze shone sharp beneath his heavy lids. "Can we then stand on Omenala and eat kola?"

"On Omenala we sit, stand, and fly. Omenala is the wing attached to our feet. It lifts us above the ground, yet we are on Ala. Omenala is the great O of the individual Chi and their movements."

From the side, Osuji's voice rose, a keen note cutting through the quiet. "Oh, once more lyric, oh music that the lame swears at his immobile limbs!"

Agbara fingers moved through the air as though drawing unseen shapes. "O, M, E, N, A, L, A — Omenala," he spelled, each letter a pulse in the silence. "O is Person, Individual. Me is Do, Deed, Action. O plus Me — Doer, Activator. N is And. Ala is Land, Planet Earth."

Ada leaned forward, "Nna anyị, Omenala is then the person and their actions which they return to?"

"Iseee!" Agbara responded, voice deep with pride. "You appeared young, yet ancestor to your mother! Yes, we stood at Omenala, yet we must stand as was willed to be repeated."

Osuji's laugh was soft, almost sorrowful. "It has been revealed; it is an endless homecoming."

"Iseee!" Agbara's voice rang again. "The Circle is the Circle; everywhere is Home. O plus Me — the individual and their deeds, or simply the person as the activator of energy that initiates a deed. Ala is what everyone in this Ama Ọcha calls the earth. Ala manifests also as the Earth God or the Invisible Dweller, she is also Alaa, place of return. At the deeper sleep of anyone, this Ama Ọcha says, Ọ lala Ụlọ. Omenala is the constant heart that takes note of every step each person takes, from the moment of birth to the return home to the soil."

Osuji's eyes were wet with memory as he spoke. "I returned from the seas, the skies."

"Yes," Agbara whispered. "Omenala does not relate exclusively to the material surface we place our feet. Omenala includes all actions taken in the visible world, be it on soil, in the deepest sea, or under the endless visible sky above. Omenala covers the tiniest observable reality to the largest apparition, because Ala governs everything observable from her domain. Since no breath is secret to Her, our actions are duly stamped in every beat of uche Obi, seat of thought and actions. Therefore, we are the activator, and our deeds are between us, Omenala."

Okeorie's voice cracked. "I wish I could free myself of the sticks that bound me!"

Agbara's eyes softened. "Nna anyị, you are free. You have come to bear witness that I speak as was given. Omenala is the mother and father of Ịlọ Ụwa — reincarnation. Maka enwedu ote mmiri shiri doo Ala amadụ. Omenala is an exhortation to hold Ọfọ, to follow the path of truth, because nothing can be hidden from the God on whose belly we place our feet every day of our lives. At the moment of deeper sleep, we return to Ala irrespective of how we chose for our earthly bodies to be disposed of — whether by fire, air, or water, we all return to the Mother's belly."

Ada's breath caught in her throat. "Nna anyị, so Omenala and Ịlọ Ụwa are interconnected?"

Agbara smiled once more. "A council of the wise, your heart will never lack."

"Iseee! Nna anyị!" Ada's voice rang out, and the crowd stirred, the air shimmering as though the trees themselves exhaled in answer.

ỊLỌỤWA
ỊLỌ - ỤWA
13+18+26
33+35+1

XIII

ỊLỌỤWA

Orie Ukwu

O Everything was as it had always been—and yet, nothing was the same. Agbara had travelled on a Dibịa's work in a land faraway. And still, all could see him. The night had fallen; the day had slipped quietly away. Day became night, night turned into the light of day. A colour crimson, blue and white, sat on branches of The Great Tree. Everyone ate, though no food had been brought to Ama Ọcha. The Great Mystic stirred, returning back into his body. No time had passed—yet the eternal dance of Chi and Abalị, of day and night, continued without pause.

Agbara's voice was soft at first, as if speaking across the veil. "Yes, Ịlọ Ụwa, Ịlọ Ụwa," his eyes gleamed, reflecting the flickering lights between the branches. "Once, in a time without time, in ebe mmadụ divided yet united into place, the I, the M, the U, and the O asked itself: Ị chọrọ Ịlọ Ụwa? It is the I, the M, the U, and the O asking Itself whether It desires to be reborn. Ịlọ is the return of the traveller. Ịlọ ụlọ, is our homecoming."

Osuji's voice broke the hush. "That is a wonder! So... the I is the M, the U, the O... It's the return of the traveler who never moved yet is everywhere."

Agbara's smile deepened, his eyes dancing. "Iseee! Ahhh, Osuji—you have touched the Eriri Ụwa—the primordial cord that binds the universe. MmỤỌ is the four parts into which the Great mụọ divides Itself. What is missing is the letter Ị of this alphabet. In this Ama Ọcha, the letter Ị indicates the second person, singular as in the phrase, Ị na-Abịa. Ụ indicates the second person plural as in, Ụnụ a na-aga? Ọ on the other hand indicates isness or that which Is as it Is, as in Ọ dịri Mma. M indicates the first-person singular or the identifier, as I call it and is seen in my Chi. So, MmỤỌ are the four ways -- ỤWaa Niile. Waa Kee Itself in many forms live various spiritual experiences that belong to the All, hence MmỤỌ or I MỤỌ.

The small m is fundamental because it holds the immanent, the Ihe kwụrụ Ihe ọdọ. Because we come from Ihe, we are MmỤỌ. Nothing can stand without its Other, or Ihe o ji the Invisible Aspect. It is Ị Ma Mmụọ, the initiation ritual a young man undergoes to know the limitless Spirit. It is the Spirit's freedom of movement in Ụwa Niile, the entire World Systems. Mmụọ travels to spaces beyond common imagination, wherever it lands, new consciousness, or forms, are born."

Osuji spoke softly, "Yet... ilo also points to hatred."

Agbara turned to him. "Yes... movement needs obstacles. Ilo is also in Iro, the contrasting realities, the Chi needs them for its evolution contrast. Such realities could be seen as negative, as in the statement, Onye ilo. Ilo needs to marry Ilu those difficulties of Ilo for its evolution. It is the mating of two complimentary entities, the Ịhụnanya necessary for both to see each other in their real nature if they appear as Mmadụ: full embodiment of Beauty. Ilo necessarily needs Ilo propulsion that permits rebirth in various worlds, including this of matter. When this happens, the individual energy then realizes its real nature: integral part of chi-ukwu, that moves with absolute freedom in all the systems of Ụwa, all the systems of the worlds."

"Nna anyị... so, we are reborn in other worlds?" Ada's voice rang out from the crowd.

"Yes, child," Agbara nodded, "It is a constant movement. If you listen well, you will hear that this Ama Ọcha calls this world Elu Ụwa and calls the world above us Elu Igwe. As everyone here knows, this Ama Ọcha is a space of temporary manifestation."

Osuji leaned forward. "So, if we keep this in mind the doors of ịlọ Ụwa open to us?"

Agbara responded, smiling, "Then shall we shine in the wisdom, we are children born into various world systems of which Ala is a part. ỊlọỤwa is a journey by which ChukwuAbịama God shines love to the world. ỊlọỤwa is a supreme act of love!"

"Can we... choose another ụwa?"

Agbara threw back his head and laughed softly. "Iseee! Osuji, you ask what your soul already knows. So, your tongue shall always rain wisdom! We are not puppets in the hands of ChukwuAbịama. Though part of the All, we maintain our individual Chi, the liberty to touch whom and where we choose, like a tree's various branches dispenses raindrops according to its length, we too move as our Chi position us at a given time."

"So... it is our ịhụnanya, our love, that draws us to a world."

"Iseee! We transform Ilo of hate to Ilo and both meet at Ịlụ, the marriage at the base of Ịhụnanya. It is one side showing its other face. Like the transformation of Otu of the number 1 into the Otu of Crowd. When Ilo of hate meets Ịlụ marry, into the Ịlọ of rebirth it births Ịhụnanya. Then it becomes a love that takes foothold and procreates in various forms, depending on the reality we travel into. When that transformation occurs and we realize ourselves as full elements of the Chineke, we are then permitted to travel into different worlds through the act of reincarnation. As can be seen then, this reincarnation is not limited to a specific world system or the immediate family circle."

Chidimma rose from the crowd. "Nna anyị Ukwu... then I could be born in China, or India, or Mexico?"

Agbara reached out as though to cup her in a blessing. "Indeed, Nne anyị! You are at total liberty of movement. Yet, imagine if Ada was not only the reincarnation of your mother, imagine her as your father, mother, sister, brother, a distant relative or the friend of a distant friend. It is this identification that solidifies ỊlọỤwa."

Osuji clapped his hands to his legs. "Ah! Hold still, my dancing foot, that I may not be found dancing to music unheard by the many!"

"Iseee!" Agbara glanced at him. "Dance, Osuji! Lift your Obi to heights uncommon! Gbaa egwu! Wrestle playfully with that impalpable visitor! Dance, dance, for, the newly arrived Energy, identified with a loved one makes reincarnation a play of the Universe. It is an act that enjoins everyone to live a life that uplifts the spirit. Because her or his memory will linger with the living when she or he is no more in this life, for, higher fruits are planted but in the heart."

A realization crossed though Osuji's body, "So, those living a few minutes from here, in Peru, in Amazonia are the reincarnations of our relative."

Ada frowned slightly, eyes wide with thought. "A few minutes from here in Peru? I know from geography that Peru and the Amazon forest are in South America."

Agbara turned, eyes twinkling as he gazed at her. "Yes, Ada. The Amazon is far... and yet, it is here. What Osuji means is that if we see those living in faraway lands as immutable parts of the Almighty Common Tree of Life, we would then be their keepers too. Knowing that a new-born is a deceased family member, we shall make sure no harm comes it. That knowledge will make us show limitless Ịhụnanya and ultimately, we shall all become keepers of our neighbours. Know you all then that ỊlọỤwa is another name for Ịfụnanya. Know you all then that the Circle is Always Complete, here, in this Ama Ọcha."

As his words faded into the hush of the night, a rain of light drifted down upon The Great Tree. One by one, the people turned, walking homeward.

And so, the gathering at Ama Ọcha became legend—a tale that passed across a thousand years. Remembered by none...except Ada.

NCHETA

NCHE - TA(A)

21+3+11+5 31+1 (1)

XIV

NCHETA

Nkwọ Ukwu

On a day after the great Dibịa spoke of Ịlọ Ụwa, the sun came home to Ama Ọcha. Everything was the same, yet all was transformed. None remembered clearly. None except Ada.

It was as if a branch, a body, or a hand unknown had stretched across the land, reaching down to grind, divide, consume, and stomach the earth at Ama Ọcha. Yet the three trees in one still stood in the heart of every home. And everyone who laid a hand upon the belly of the great tree seemed to remember, from a fluttering petal or a raindrop, till the end of time, some events that happened in the square.

But the great Dibịa was nowhere to be found.

Ada went to the compound, her absence, a present. She seated herself at the mouth—the only entrance and exit to the underground Obi. And there she remained, from Eke Ukwu to Nkwọ Ukwu and back again to Eke Nta.

Otu, the number one, became AsaAtọ, number eight—seven folded into three, yet solidly rooted in the perfect circle of eight. Otu Ọnwa soon went into Otu Afọ, weeks danced into months, one year became ten and to the infinite. None, not brother, mother, father, uncle, granduncle or aunt could move Ada.

She remembered that which none knew clearly.

She sat in bliss, radiating immense light, refusing to open her mouth—and yet, she spoke. None understood her. None except Okechi. Her locks had grown white as freshly tapped palm wine, twisting into roots that curled and entwined into dwarf palm trees, forming a living circle around the mouth of the Obi. People came from near and far to behold the girl who had become one with the trees. Countless branches cradled birds and butterflies that multiplied, aged, and renewed themselves.

Then, one day, when Okechi—no longer a boy, but a man with a wife and children—spoke in anger, his words struck something deep in Ada, no longer a child, yet daughter to the very earth she rested on. Ada opened her mouth. The entire world that had gathered around formed a semicircle at the mouth of the Obi, drawn to the sound.

Okechi's voice trembled with anger and confusion. "Ada Nne anyị, Ncheta seems as nails that pierce Obi; in this Obi... could the dwellers in the world of Ncheta unsettle the present?"

Ada's voice was soft but resonant, as if the trees themselves were speaking. "Know, Okechi, that Ncheta is a dance of energies. There is no conflict. Nche is to guard. Taa is today—as everyone in this Obi knows. Together, Nche and Taa becomes Ncheta—memory. But memory is not dormant, no, no... memory does not belong to the past."

Okechi's brow furrowed, his voice thick. "Ada Nne anyị ... so memory doesn't belong to the past?"

A faint smile crossed Ada's face, her eyes shining with light. "Iseee! Ncheta is an invitation to guard today, our deeds now, because they rise from the past and yet they are the present and belong to the future. See this Obi—it was here yesterday, it is here today, it will be here tomorrow, even when it is physically brought down. Ncheta called you all here. Every action taken here will live in the Obi, the heart of everyone. Ncheta is the guard, the eye, the ear, and the mouth of an everlasting Taa."

A child's voice rang out—Udechi, four and eight, daughter of Okechi, the return of Chidimma herself. Her small hands clasped in wonder. "Nne anyị Ukwu, so the past and present are two faces that meet in Ncheta?"

Ada's laughter was like the rustling of the palms. "Iseee, Nne m Ọma! You speak ancient wisdom. Nche needs Taa to become Ncheta. The living are called to become guardians, not only of the past but of today, for today is the foundation of Echi—the energy of tomorrow."

She leaned forward, her voice a whisper that reached every heart. "Nne m ọma, i gee ntị nke ọma, ị ga-anụ na Ncheta na Echi na-ada otu. They are interlinked. Because the past and present meet in the now, they are two faces of an inseparable coin as you revealed. Chee Taata Nche, maka Echi is an ancient invitation to conscious living. It takes the living to remember the past, and a thing is in the past the moment they are manifest. Guard or be conscious of the actions of the moment, for then sweetly will it sound in the future."

Okechi's voice softened, now reverent. "This Obi was here yesterday, is here today, will be here tomorrow. And whatever is remembered springs from the actions carefully executed here. Every moment... is Ncheta."

Ada's eyes shone like twin moons. "Iseee! Because the circle is always complete."

DIBỊA
DI - BỊA
4+12
(1)+2+13+1

XIV

DIBỊA

Nkwọ Ukwu

O Dikeakọ rose from among the gathered Otu -- a great assembly before Ada. He remembered Ada—not merely as a daughter once cradled in his arms, but as sister, mother, grandmother, all at once. With solemn grace, Dikeakọ approached and offered a kola nut to Ada, now sage, radiant with wisdom beyond time.

She sat in stillness, silent for a span longer than time itself. Yet as the hush deepened, her voice fell upon every heart, as clear and gentle as falling rain.

"Ụmụm, ana m anabata onye ọwụla n'ime m, maka ụnụ niile, ma nwoke ma nwaanyị wụ nwam, ụnụ niile wụ ụmụ Ada. I am welcoming each of you inside me, because everyone, man or woman, is my child, the children of Ada." She spoke without parting her lips, yet all heard her—felt her. And in that moment, each soul present was cradled like a long-lost child pressed once more to a mother's bosom. For whom, as a true child, could ever forget the bosom that once fed them?

Ada lifted her head, received Dikeakọ's gifts, and bowed to him with deep respect—forever father, yet son to her.

Dikeakọ's voice trembled, heavy with yearning. "Ada, where then is the great Dibịa? Has he died? And if he did, where is the body? Has he reincarnated into another world? Adam, who then is the Dibịa?"

"Nna anyị, a Dibịa never dies. Listen to the word, for therein lies the truth: di-bịa. Dibịa is the I Am that Is here yet Comes. A simultaneous presence and absence. The Dibịa, who she is, and yet is not."

Her voice wove through the assembly like a current in the wind. "Listen to the *Di* you hear in *Ihe Di Ala Mma*. The *Bịa* in *Bịa n'Ogbe Anyị*, or in *Onye ọBịa*. Di is presence, essence, here-ness. Bịa is coming, returning, going. The Dibịa can be in different places at once. Dibịa is ubiquity manifested."

"Ọ dị mma, Ada!" Okechi, standing tall among the people, exclaimed.

"Iseee! You have spoken wisely," She smiled at him. "Ọ dị mma—it is beautiful. Yet you have expressed an ancient truth, known in all world systems. Ọ dị mma: It is beautiful. It is what I know. What you have uttered is the universe proclaiming, it is what I know to be beautiful. I am beautiful. The universe, in all its forms, is an expression of mma—beauty absolute."

Her gaze swept the assembly. "Follow the words; therein lay the code to the mystery. The Dibịa is not dead and is never so. The Dibịa goes into what some call Astral or full body Time travel. Onye Di ma na-Abịa nwere ike ịhụ ihe niile e zoro ezo."

A small figure stepped forward—Uche, little son of Okechi, his eyes round with curiosity. He reached up and whispered into Ada's ear. "Dààdà, where is the Dibịa hiding?"

Ada gathered Uche into her arms, her voice a gentle tide that washed over not just the child but the entire Otu.

"Uche, the Dibịa is not hiding. He has simply chosen to be away in the body. The Dibịa is at ease with sun, moon, air, rain—the visible and the invisible. And when the Dibịa is called, when he is willed to daa the people see him and cry out with joy: Ọbịa-la, Ọbatala! The universe, he, she, has arrived, come, landed. And when he leaves, young and old, elders and sages dance and nod in agreement, some singing, Ọ la-ala—he has gone, returned to the land; others, Ọ pụọla—he has gone out, he has germinated." The germination here refers to all the systems of the worlds and their various growths of peculiar trees of life. The systems in which the Dibịa travels to in his work of espousing various practices, as willed by the inhabitants and in accordance with the Universal law of *pụta,* manifestation on a given day.

Listen deeper and hear, dance to the mysterious music of, *Ọ bịa-Ala.* The Dibịa merges coming and going into a simultaneous, endless dance to create *O me n'Ala,* according to the needs of the land, people and the period. And when this Ọ Bị a ALa, this, Coming, Landing that is also Going happens, new worlds, realities, consciousness are born, existing ones reinforced, so that the Dibịa moves with ease into other realms where he is expected. It is known that humans have the Chi; the Dibịa is the one that puts into practice this Essence, thereby becoming a direct messenger of God. The Dibịa is like a Dancer of the Worlds and wherever he places his feet new seeds are sowed, old dead flowers take life and blossom."

All fell still as her final words hung in the air because "The Circle is Always Complete."

AZỤ
A - Z - Ụ
1 37 33

XVI

AZỤ

Eke Nta

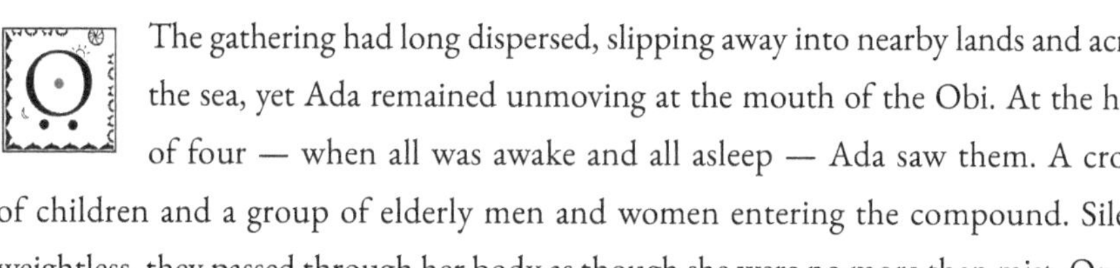

The gathering had long dispersed, slipping away into nearby lands and across the sea, yet Ada remained unmoving at the mouth of the Obi. At the hour of four — when all was awake and all asleep — Ada saw them. A crowd of children and a group of elderly men and women entering the compound. Silent, weightless, they passed through her body as though she were no more than mist. One by one they disappeared into the earth, into the belly of the underground Obi.

Voices then rose from the underground and filled the compound in powerful tangible waves. It was then that Ada stirred. Rising, she walked with measured steps to the Obi beneath the earth. The Obi had four, formerly invisible doors that opened revealing a garden unlike any Ada had known. Dwarf irokos, pregnant dwarf breadfruit trees, giant pears, sky-reaching palm trees and timbers of unknown origins towered in the garden, all so alien yet familiar and homely.

Birds and butterflies flew from the belly of the earth and towered above the skies. Serpents, monkeys, leopards, known and unknown creatures lived, dancing blissfully in the garden that opened up before Ada's eyes. From behind a colossal breadfruit tree emerged Agbara, the great Dibịa. He had grown long, dark locks that shimmered like a river of night. His face, neither young nor old, holding a strange eternal youthfulness. Behind him, the pregnant palms glowed, their fruits luminous, casting golden light through the four doors.

Agbara's eyes lifted to Ada, and a smile, gentle and knowing, touched his lips. He nodded welcome to his stunned guest. Ada's eyes searched for the visitors, but they had gone. She saw, then, the moment of their transformation — how they had become one with the trees, their spirits now entwined with bark, root, and leaf. Bowing her head in reverence, Ada stepped forward as Agbara gestured for her to sit beside him.

Though his mouth barely moved, his voice poured forth, a steady stream flowing into the heart of the garden. Ada drank, sure then she was called to water the Otu, as they would appear.

"Nna anyị," Ada murmured softly, "anya m jiri hụ gị a kpọkwala m ishi."

"Your eyes shall never be blinded, Adam," he responded, "But why this wonderment? Was I not there when you preached the Dibịa's sermon?"

Ada's lips curved into a wry smile. "Nna anyị, we beg our eyes sometimes. For that which we think we know hides behind our backs. Then do we not know if we are Azụ of buying, Ire of the seller or the Ịzụ of the breeder, tending that was already grown."

Agbara leaned back. "Adam, Iseee to your Obi, your Ire, Ntị, and Anya. You have married heart, tongue, ears, and eyes into one. Now you speak of Azụ — staring deep into simple words great truths are unravelled."

Ada inclined her head. "I mena, Nna anyị."

"Azụ is then back, fish, feed, buy, sell," Agbara continued. "There is little variation between the Azụ of back or fish. But Azụ, like the sun on this Osisi Nkwụ, mothers many offspring, each wandering its own path. Azụ, like a hand, indiscriminately nurtures, trades, sells what is bred. It is like Ire — the tongue that speaks healing and damnation. In fact, therein lay a tightening chord, a rope that could lead to buying and selling, to slavery. Azụ and Ire are endowed with creative and destructive qualities. Both are connected and when married on a negative bed produces, Ire Azụ Mmadụ Onye n'azụ na-ere Mmadu. The constant combination of both could lead to a system that normalizes inhumanity. Azụ Ire Mmadu."

Ada shivered. "Like speaking from the back of the tongue..."

"Iseee! Yes, Ada. The back of a person's tongue or buy a human being. Speaking from the back of the tongue — that is evil. For the tongue, chief priest of the word, is meant to be rooted in truth. On the other hand, Onye na-Azụ nwa/mmadụ. It also means, one who is buying a human being. Anọ m gị n'Azụ. Eso m gị n'Azụ.

Be careful, child, for the one behind you is not always the one who wants to sell you. Azụ onye dị mma is an expression that exposes treacherous tongues. On the other hand, Anọ m gị n'Azụ expresses the original human spirit of support. Because, Azụ is deeply rooted on Ịhụnanya for MmaDụ, the Beauty that is the Human Being. Is it not said that to feed an entire population you show them how to fish?"

Ada's voice was quiet, reverent. "Take away the spinal cord, and Mmadụ becomes a jelly mass."

"Iseee! Because the Circle is always complete, Adam."

SI/SỌ
EKWENSU
EKWE - NSU/NSI/NSỌ
5+17+5
21+29+32/21+29+12/21+29+26

XVI

EKWENSU

Afọ Ukwu

O Eke traversed Orie, danced into Afọ, and became Nkwọ. Ada and Agbara sat in the circle of Nka-ta, the gathering of knowing and presence. Bones, wood, stones, and leaves seemed to stir from the great Dibịa's face, shaping themselves into words perceived only by Ada.

Yet amid this dance of elements, the great Mystic emanated silence. Ada, in turn, shone from the ihe, the light of wisdom expressed in images. The new became old, the old reborn as new. The Dibịa discarded his skin and so did Ada. They entered a space where one plus one was two, yet greater than three, for the non-manifest shows its face but to a few.

On an evening of Afọ, when Orie was traded and what was bought and sold at Eke had been ground and made flesh in Afa, Ada appeared again at the mouth of the Obi. Still deep in communion with the Mystic, she met a multitude unexpected.

Her locks, a multitude of umbilical cords, extended from her crown towards the Dibịa. She glowed with Ihe— the purest Light — so brilliant it seemed the sun itself had come to bed upon her head. The crowd drank from her light and she drank from theirs. Children played with her locks until she spoke, her words few, yet the meanings long.

Uche was the first to step forward, his young face lifted in earnest wonder.

"Daada," he began, "my teacher once rose in anger against my classmate and pronounced, Ekwensu kpọọ gị ọkụ! Ekwensu should burn you! But... my mother says Ekwensu is not a bad spirit. She says Ekwensu would never harm a child. Is my mother right?"

Ada's eyes softened. "Ah, Uche... you ask a riddle older than the fathers of your fathers. Your mother is right. Ekwensu is a name full of riddles, like many others in this Obi. Some of the riddles are accessible through the word. Ekwe is the drum of Ekwere m. It is the root of the Belief in Ihe dị Nsọ, Nsu, Nsi. It navigates the world of Holiness, the system of beliefs in that which is Holy, sacred. But, as in all things, there is duality. Nsi, is also present in a dormant form in Ekwensu. If we deal openly and from the world of the sacred, the Nsi will transform to Nzu and from thence will shine the sacred light of Holiness."

Dikeakọ stepped forward, his voice deep. "Adam, does it mean that Ekwensu dwells where we place it?"

Ada smiled. "Iseee, Nna m. Ekwensu is like a lamp. If you light it, its glow showers the world. Place it in darkness, and it will hide, swallowed by blindness. It is where we place the lamps of our words. Imagine a person whose real name is hidden, replaced with another. Soon the person or thing will begin to respond to the new name that will slowly define its identity. That is the power of Okwu — the power of the Word. Okwu and Ụka can mean word, wisdom, or quarrel. Words assume the specific meaning a people give to it."

Chidimma tilted her head, her eyes bright. "Adam... is that why it's said, Arụshi kpaa nganga, ezi ya oshishi e jiri pịaa ya?"

"Iseee, Nne m. it is so," she responded, "If an Arụshi misbehaves we will show it the wood from which it was carved. Iseee! The spirit you infuse into a word will soon become its physical reality, because thoughts and words are tangible. In Ekwensu we hear the Drum of Holiness or of Nsi depending on where we place our lamp. Yet all is originally pure Mma, pure Beauty. If Mmadụ dwells in Di in the Isness of Mma, everything around will then manifest that original Beauty, the purpose of the journey of manifestation on earth. Ekwensu Bi n'Ihe and needs to be lit for the glow to shine on all."

Uche frowned, wrestling with the thought. "Daada, anahụ m aghọta, Ekwensu ọ wụdụ ajọ Mmụọ? I don't understand. Is Ekwensu not the devil?"

Ada reached for his small hands, cradling them in hers. "Ekwensu Is — wherever the Obi, the heart, abides in any moment. Ekwensu is part of the infinite wisdom of all things. Uche Obi, as shaped in the heart, manifests what is believed. When your father or mother says I believe in God, they say, Ekwere m na Chineke, Chukwu. So, reality manifests according to what is believed at a given time.

Your mother knows and will feed you more as you proceed. Ekwere m na Chukwu, is a common form of declaring I believe in God. Gee ntị nke ọma, I ga anụ na Ekwere nọọ n'ime Ekwensu. If you listen well, you will hear that ekwere – belief, is in Ekwensu.

Otu onye chọrọ ịmata ma ndị ha ekwetara ihe ọ na-ekwu, ọ ga-asị Igbo Kwe nu! Belief amongst your fellow humans is in fact the search for the light of truth. Ekwensu Is not the Devil, yet could well Be for a person, according to ebe O Bi. Nsu is also Nzu, the purest of chalk with which truth is drawn out and made manifest in various physical forms.

Ekwensu Is in harmony with the Holy O, Circle of the Universe. Wherever one positions their Nzu, however one throws or draws their Nzu takes away nothing from the nature of the chalk of manifestation.

The circle," Ada whispered, her words a blessing, "is always complete."

As her words faded into the evening hush, the children slipped from her locks. Parents called. Feet shuffled, and the multitude dispersed in joy, their hearts lighter for the truths carried home.

Ada remained seated at the mouth of the Obi, the last light glancing off her brow. She watched, silent, as the first circle of Nka Taa came to its end — only to turn, as all circles do, into a new beginning.

End of the First Circle

PostScript

First Circle

I Birth the Spiritual Art of Conversation Today

It is essential to explain that numbers are of fundamental importance in entering the portal of the cosmology, metaphysics and philosophy encoded in the Igbo language. In this first circle, I introduce numbers first, and subsequently letters; letters being the instruments used to give sound to words. Yet, it is not my intention to establish a superiority between numbers and letters. Therefore, I interchange between numbers and letters as (M) = (I) am led to + (Mụọ) = Birth/Deliver + (Nka) = Art + (Taa) = Today moves me to birth/deliver the spiritual, art of conversation today.

The harmonious dance of numbers and letters is evidenced by listening to the Igbo word, Daa (sound) Land. Daa is the "word/sound" used to express this melodious movement of "landing/dropping/falling." "Sound" being so expressed is not abstract but a tangible entity, because only a thing with, "ahụ/arụ (body)" would "land."

This concept is properly expressed in the saying of some parts of Igbo land, in the phrase "ote(o) ihe shi ada" or "ụda ihe/ife". From an immediate translation, this phrase is simply rendered as, "the way a thing/light lands or the sound of a thing/light." As a way of showing the method of this work, I am going to "dissect" the phrase by using numbers and simple Latin letters:

24+30 +5 = O+T+E(e) = OTE(e)

To move a step further, I will carry out a "division/separation" of two syllables in "ote" and correlate them to the last letters of the sentence. Therefore, the first and the last, interestingly show the last to be intrinsically linked to the first.

O+TE(o) = OTE(o). I will clarify the subject of O+TE= OTE Ihe shi A+DA(a)=ADA/DAA/Falls/Lands (How a Thing Lands) this way: O/E=A of Ada(a). The first O/Universe is therefore equal to the Fallen/Landed A/Ada (a). This way you have the first in the last and vice versa, because the Circle is always Complete.

The last letter "e" is silent and is never conventionally written, but the statement shows what is being expressed. O TE(e) says: "O" has "awoken." The "O" in question being the "Universe," the perfect "Zero" a Dibịa draws in the Obi (Heart/Home) every time the mystic goes into "ịtụ ogu/ịgba afa," (communes/wrestles/converses/divines between himself/herself and the Almighty Ụwa niile/Universe.)

"Ihe/Ife" is Light while "Ada" is famously known to be the First Daughter, and "Daa" is "Fall" yet an appellation of respect towards a woman. The sentence therefore talks of how the Woken Cosmic Light Daa/Falls/Lands into the first daughter "Ada" so life, light, sound and every form becomes possible. This is a mandate that points to Ada Birthing/Landing our Chi/Light (the Universe birthing Itself in this consciousness). Not only that, it refers to the moment our individual Chi plucks/picks Its own Ihe/Ife/ Light, detaches from Ụwa Niile (Universe), and Daa/Be-comes/Lands into this plane of Gravity. This is at the inception when everything, including Sound, Is at the stage of "Be/Beingness/Wholeness," detaching and Daa/Landing/Coming into physicality here. Sound travels everywhere simultaneously and this capacity of being in one place while n'Ala/ comes/goes home into various lands, is a Universal statement of Ubiquity. So, for the Chi of Sound to Daa/Land, it needs to be willed into physical shape and that form is shown in numbers, letters, and many other forms of physical representation, as the need and culture may require.

Interestingly, "Otu" as the number "1/I" also means Group/Conference/Meeting. Independent of the letter/symbol used to represent it; the first sound with which the Universal "Λ/E/I/M/O/U" announces It-Self in the sentence is "O", exactly in one of its forms which is circular. Daa, therefore, tells us that "sound" is tangible, and the physicality can be expressed in "numbers". Therefore, sound and number are two faces of a larger coin. Daa goes further to show that the ancient Igbos were present when Everything was O(tu)/One/1/Circular/Whole, and landing/surfacing on planet Earth, the All found numbers, letters and various others, as forms of physical representation.

I am compelled to explain the irregular use I am going to make of the capital letter in the Igbo alphabet of "Mm". As will be shown in this work, I am going to separate the first capital "M" from the small "m", therefore creating an extra number of letters in the Igbo alphabet as it is commonly used. This is necessary because "M" is both the pronoun "I" and the possessive pronoun "Me/Mine". In a word, the separate capital M is the identifier, the Universe expressing Itself as female. "M" in this work represents female energy and is properly expressed in the word M=Me/Myself +mụọ=birth/deliver. "Mmụọ" therefore fully expresses the concept of self-birth or auto-regeneration. This concept is shown by the M=Energy of the Universe that mụọ/births/manifests in various forms in entire world systems. The physical act of delivering is indisputably carried out in the female body in this Ala/Earth consciousness and Ala is the Igbo word for Earth/Land.

Here then, is the Igbo alphabet and the numbers I associate with them in this work:

A = 1
B = 2
C = 3
D = 4
E = 5
F = 6
G = 7
Gb = 8
Gh = 9
Gw = 10
H = 11
I = 12
Ị = 13
J = 14
K = 15
Kp = 16
Kw = 17
L = 18

M = 19
Mm = 20
N = 21
Ṅ = 22
Nw = 23
Ny = 24
O = 25
Ọ = 26
P = 27
R = 28
S = 29
Sh = 30
T = 31
U = 32
Ụ = 33
V = 34
W = 35
Y = 36
Z = 37

ỌGỤ ỌNỤ

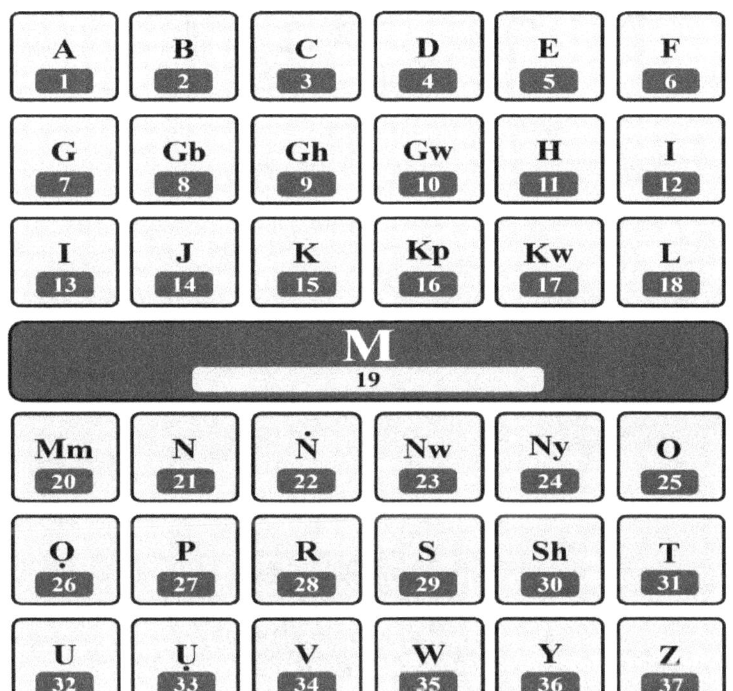

THE FIRST EDITION OF

MMỤỌ NKATA

ENCOUNTERS IN IGBO LANGUAGE

BY

ALFIE M. NZE

2025

www.ingramcontent.com/pod-product-compliance
Lightning Source LLC
LaVergne TN
LVHW010616110826
845149LV00003B/933